PART I
UNCONDITIONAL

When I was fourteen, my mother told me there was no such thing as unconditional love.

"I could stop loving you at any time," my mother said.

We were folding laundry. A sheet, her on one end, me on the other. Together, like old-fashioned dancers, we brought our hands together to bisect the long white sheet, then stepped toward each other, the fabric collapsing inward, and then again, then once more, until the long, tangled mess was sorted into a sleek, flat rectangle. It was warm from the dryer and smelled like chemical flowers.

"No one loves without conditions," she said.

I nodded and set aside the sheet, reached into the basket for another. I snapped it out and she caught the far end.

"Your father's love for me is conditional," she continued. "His love is contingent on lots of things. My willingness to listen to him talk about his day. My cooking."

We came together. At fourteen, I was now as tall as she was. "And my beauty."

"Your beauty?"

"Love for a woman," my mother said, "is always conditional on her beauty. That," she said, my fingers grazing hers on the final fold, "and sex."

2

She was sorting out the truth of things for me, much as we together smoothed the wrinkles from the sheets, taking something lengthy and burdensome and rearranging it into a neat package.

"Of course," she said, "My love for your father has conditions, too."

I knew without her telling me what some of these conditions were. The money he made in real estate. His deference to her preferences, like the new car purchased every three years, whether the last one needed replacing or not. His donning of the black-and-white striped apron each Sunday afternoon, then going into the backyard to light the grill in the outdoor kitchen. The way he cooked her meat—soft in the middle, dripping red.

"What could make you stop loving me?" I asked.

"Oh, any number of things," she said. "But you would never do any of them, so it doesn't matter."

I wanted to know what they were, the unlisted cardinal sins. But she would not tell me.

"It's a ridiculous question," she said, stacking the folded sheets into the basket and thrusting it toward me.

The basket was heavy. I took it.

《《《

There would have been other kids, after me. I remember my mother's pregnancies, nearly one a year from when I was five until when I turned ten, when I suppose she decided enough was enough. Each of those pregnancies ended the same way—early.

She usually didn't look any different, between when she was pregnant and when she wasn't. I knew there was a baby

3

when her favorite glass disappeared before dinner—squat, clear crystal, filled with two fingers of vodka and topped with diet tonic water. I knew the baby was gone when her favorite glass reappeared.

She stopped telling me about the pregnancies after the second miscarriage, and then I learned to notice on my own when the cup disappeared, understanding that its disappearance meant there was another baby inside of her.

It was clear that we weren't supposed to talk about the pregnancies. Bad luck, I guess? So I didn't, but each time the glass disappeared, I would make up names and stories and decide if it was a girl or a boy. The second-to-last pregnancy, when I was eight years old, progressed to the point where it seemed kind of silly not to say anything. She was puffing out, and her stomach was bigger—not hard big like the pregnant ladies I'd see out in the world, but definitely bigger.

That one, I'd decided, was a girl. A sister. I named her Chloe, because I liked fancy names like that, and because I thought it sounded good tagged after mine. Nina and Chloe. Sisters. She would have reddish hair. And she'd need glasses, like me. I would be the one to figure it out, that she was near-sighted; I'd take care of her all the time, after all, so I'd be the first to notice that something wasn't right with her vision, the way she'd cling to me, afraid to venture on her own. We'd get her some of those really cute baby glasses, purple, with a flexible frame and the extra-long ear parts that tuck all the way around, not just right behind the ears like mine. Chloe would be kind of fat, but that would be okay, because she'd only be a baby and she would have plenty of time to grow out of it. Fat is cute, on babies. I would share a room with her. I wouldn't need to; our house was plenty big, but I'd *want* to.

She would be *my* person, not my mother's or father's. She would be my person to love.

But then one night the crystal glass was out again, just like the other times. I remember feeling sick, like I had the flu, and I said I wasn't hungry and went straight to bed. My mother never said anything to me about it, and I never said anything to her.

When the glass disappeared again the next year, I didn't make up any names. I just waited for it to reappear again, and when it did, just a few weeks later, I was glad.

There's a refrigerator somewhere. It's a white refrigerator, with French doors and a pull-out freezer at the bottom, because those are the fanciest refrigerators.

This refrigerator, when you pull open the doors, both at the same time, and you throw them wide to peer inside— it's filled with cartons and cartons of eggs. Each shelf holds cartons stacked like bricks, one atop another, rows and rows of them, and each carton holds twelve eggs. No more, no less. Always twelve.

And the eggs inside the cartons . . . they are smooth and they are white and they are perfect. Sometimes when you buy eggs from the grocery store (especially the organic kind) they are flecked with dried chicken shit. But these eggs are so clean as to seem bleached. How could it be that these eggs have been pushed through the slit of a worried hen? How could it be that these eggs are the product of a bird's bodily function?

But they are. These eggs are the collected oeuvre of one hen, a nervous leghorn called Rose for the bright-red comb upon her head.

Red is the comb upon her head. White are the feathers upon her wings, clipped straight across to prevent her from flying. White are the eggs she lays, day after day after day after day.

Lay, lie, lay. She lays her eggs. They lie in the nesting box. She lies upon them, waiting, hoping. The farmer sneaks a hand beneath her warm white feathers to snatch the eggs. He does not bother with lies or promises. She will lay more, just the same, without a lie.

Does she miss her eggs? Did she love them? It doesn't matter. Her life is to lay and lie and lay again. The eggs fill the cartons and the cartons fill the fridge, and the white French doors seal them tightly away.

Once upon a time, chickens laid eggs only during mating season, only as many eggs as the hens could manage were they to become chicks. But the farmer wanted more— more eggs for his omelets, more eggs to take to market. More, more, more. And so the farmers and the scientists chose the chickens who were the very best producers and selected them for breeding, to make hens who laid even more eggs, and so on and so on. And now a hen can lay an egg almost every day. She can lay three hundred eggs a year, in her best laying years, and she can keep laying eggs for years to come—up to a thousand eggs. A thousand eggs the hen can lay, and then, when she cannot lay any more, she can still give—she can lie on the roasting pan, and lie on the table, and the farmer and his family, with a fridge full of a thousand eggs behind them, can carve her open at the table, and when they have finished their supper they can find one thing more—a bone, her wishbone—and the laughing farmer's children can grasp it with hands still oily from her meat, and they can wish and they can break it into two.

"Ms. Faye."

I look up. I had been fooling around on my phone, not that there was anything interesting on it, just to disappear as much as I could. I'd driven myself there, to the Costa Mesa Planned Parenthood, which was a joke of a name because no one went there planning for parenthood, they all went planning for un-parenthood.

There isn't a Planned Parenthood in Irvine, where we live. Irvine, California. Named the safest city in America, two years in a row. Safest for fetuses, too, I guess, since we don't have any abortion clinics at all. You have to go to Santa Ana or Costa Mesa for that.

I hate driving. It scares me, especially driving to new places. I don't drive very far, usually—I have my set schedule that takes me to predictable places at predictable times. Irvine is utterly predictable. It's what they call a "planned community," meaning that each neighborhood was developed by a builder. So each neighborhood has a name and a feeling. A theme. Orchard Hills, Irvine Grove, The Colony. Like the different lands in Disneyland—Tomorrowland, Fantasyland.

We live in Shady Canyon. It's not that shady, and there's no canyon.

When my parents handed me the keys to my car last spring on my sixteenth birthday, a three-year-old Toyota Prius that Mom had picked out for herself during her "global awareness" phase, they made me promise that I wouldn't drive on freeways. This wasn't a hard promise to make since freeways scare the crap out of me. But I broke that promise, today, to come here.

I tuck my phone into my jacket pocket and stand. Follow the nurse. Maybe she is a nurse. She's wearing scrubs, anyway, so she must do something medical.

She weighs me first, and measures me. Average. I filled out the forms in the waiting room, and I hesitated over the birth date, considering making myself a little older, like eighteen or nineteen, even though I know from their website that they won't turn me away for being young. But I ended up being honest, because maybe it would matter somehow, my age, for the dosage or something.

Then she hands me one of those blue paper "gowns," they call them, which is a joke, and tells me to leave it open in the front for the breast exam.

"There's nothing wrong with my breasts," I tell her.

She smiles. It's a nice smile. "I'm sure there isn't, honey, but this is a well-woman exam. We routinely check for breast abnormalities along with doing a Pap smear. Okay?"

Sure. Why not? As long as they're at it, what's a little boob play, between friends?

"Is this your first time?"

I look up, embarrassed.

"For an exam," she clarifies.

"Oh. Yeah. It is."

"It'll be fine," she says. "Just get changed. The nurse-practitioner will be in soon."

After the door closes behind her, I consider placing the still-folded paper gown on the exam table and just getting the hell out of there. But then I picture Seth's brown eyes, the way they look up at me from between my thighs, and I stay.

My clothes form a growing pile on the chair by the door. Boots. Socks. Jeans and underwear, yanked down together. Flannel shirt. Tank. Bra.

I'm cold. On second thought, I pluck the socks from the pile. They couldn't need to see my feet, too. Feet have nothing to do with it.

The paper gown is as stupid and uncomfortable as it looked, but at least my socks are still warm.

I perch on the end of the exam table, waiting. I wait for fifteen minutes.

Finally I figure they've forgotten about me. I scoot off the table and am just about to get dressed and leave when the door finally opens.

"Sorry to keep you waiting," says the woman. As she enters the room, she squirts sanitizer from a jar by the door and rubs her hands together. She's wearing a white coat over black slacks and a gray blouse. "Complications." She doesn't elaborate, just motions for me to climb back up on the table.

She's Asian, and younger than my mother. She isn't pretty, but I don't need her to be pretty. She has, I notice, small hands. In this current situation, small hands seem radically more important than pretty.

She has my chart in her small hands. It's basically just a folder with a single piece of paper inside. I'd filled out the paper in the waiting room. Name: Nina Faye. Date of Birth: May 25. Age: 16. Sexually Active? Yes.

Other questions follow—the first day of my last period, the

type of birth control I am currently using, history of sexually transmitted diseases. I checked all the boxes honestly, though I flinched to admit that I didn't use birth control. That is why I am here, after all—to get on the Pill. Or maybe to get that shot. Though I hate needles.

She looks up from the chart.

"You're here for birth control?"

"Yes."

"The shot?"

"No," I say, certain, suddenly. "The Pill."

"The shot is safer. You can't forget to take it."

I shrug. Say nothing.

She sighs and pinches the top of her nose, just beneath her glasses. Then she looks again at my file. "It says here you're not currently using any birth control, but that you're sexually active."

I want to kick myself for not checking the other box.

"You know, the Pill will prevent pregnancy, but it won't do anything about sexually transmitted diseases. AIDS, herpes, genital warts . . . the Pill won't stop any of that."

I look right into her eyes and don't blink or answer, and after a second she looks down. "Okay," she says.

She washes her hands and then snaps on a pair of gloves. "We'll start with listening to your lungs."

I want to ask a question, just to relieve my tension, but she fits the stethoscope into her ears and I become a patient.

"Breathe in," she says. "And out." I empty myself of air, making myself hollow, imagining myself blowing out not just the air but my thoughts, as well, and picture everything else following afterwards: my stomach, my intestines, my blood and heart, and my lungs themselves, turned inside out by my exhalation.

We have a stethoscope at home. I don't know why, or where

it came from. It has been there as long as I remember. As a child I would creep away with it and listen for the heartbeat in my stuffed animals. Sometimes, when my parents' bedroom door was closed and locked, I'd press the stethoscope up against the door to hear the sounds inside. Not words. Not crying, either—something else.

I remember the sounds now, suddenly and perfectly, though I haven't thought of them in many years. It's the stethoscope, round and warm like a mouth against my back, and the reason I'm here on this table that bring the sounds back to me.

"All clear," she says. "Now we'll examine your breasts."

She works her way around my left breast first, what little breast I have, making concentric passes with her fingertips. If I let it, it would feel kind of good. When she gets to the nipple, she squeezes it a little. I breathe in sharply. I wasn't expecting that.

"Do you examine your breasts at home?" she asks, moving on to the right one.

"Umm . . . no."

"It's easy to do," she says. "You just work your way around, like I'm doing, checking for anything unusual, like lumps. In the shower is a great place. Soap and water helps your hands glide more smoothly. Lay back," she says, and I do, and she lifts my arm up over my head and explores my armpit a little, push-ing here and there. "Fine," she says. "Perfectly normal."

I start to sit up but she puts a hand on my chest, just above my breasts. "Just lie down," she says, "and scoot your bottom down toward the end of the table. Put your feet in the stirrups."

Okay. Not surprising, but still. Not exactly comfortable. My heels are cupped in the hard plastic stirrups; the paper gown bunches up as I shift lower on the table.

"Scoot down a little more."

I scoot.

"A little more."

I feel like I'm about to slide off the table and into her lap. It's awful.

"Now we'll do the pelvic exam," she says. "Just relax."

She switches out her gloves for a fresh pair. "First I'll examine your vulva," she says. "Would you like a mirror?"

Maybe the only thing that could make this situation even more embarrassing would be to have a mirror in my hand right now. "No thanks."

"You should look at your vulva and vagina regularly," she tells me, and I imagine her at home, with a glass of wine, rubbing her breasts and taking vaginal selfies.

Her fingers feel nothing like Seth's. There's nothing erotic about her touch, but at least it doesn't take long. "Perfectly normal," she tells me. For a half second I think we're done when she turns away, but then she picks something up from the metal tray next to her and I know I'm not getting out of here that easily.

She pulls a plastic thing out of its sealed plastic wrapping and smears some clear jelly stuff on the tip. "This is a speculum. I use it to open your vagina so I can see your cervix more clearly. It won't hurt," she says, "though it may feel a bit uncomfortable." Then she says again, "Just relax," and I feel the cold nosing tip of the speculum against the entrance of my vagina, totally different from the press of Seth's warm, hard penis but still not that different, really.

Then I hear the speculum ratchet open and I'm more exposed than I've ever been. There's a bright light shining between my legs like I'm on frigging Broadway or something and all her energy totally focused on the inside of my vagina. I look up at the ceiling.

Kittens. There are pictures of kittens, torn from magazines, dotting the ceiling above the exam table. "Hang in there!" encourages one kitten from a thought bubble. It clings to a branch by its claws. "It's nothing purr-sonal!" claims another. This one lies curled and content in a pet bed, with a large sad-eyed dog looking on.

"Perfect. No lesions or sores," she says, which I hadn't even realized was something she'd be looking for. "Now I'll take a few cells from your cervix for the Pap smear." She holds up a little brush and dips back down to insert it. I can feel the brush scraping against the inside of me, my cervix, I guess.

She's done now and she's cranking down the speculum and pulling it out. There's a weird gooey sound and a brief feeling of being emptied out, like a vacuum. I wonder if I look any different down there now, after having been stretched by that thing. Then I think of all the vaginas in the world that have pushed out babies, and I figure probably the speculum is pretty minor in the grand scheme of Things Put Into Vaginas.

"I'll give you a minute to get dressed," she says, pulling her gloves off inside out. "Then we'll talk more about birth control options." The gloves go in the bin marked MEDICAL WASTE next to the door on her way out, as though the touch of me—of my vagina—is toxic.

≪≪≪

Twice a week after school, Tuesdays and Thursdays, I volunteer at a high-kill shelter. Every time I'm there, I see the conditions under which people determine love.

Youth + symmetry + quietness = love

Young dogs find homes quickly. Old dogs are fucked. Dogs who are missing something—an eye, a leg? They lack symmetry. It's lethal injection for them, almost all the time. Barkers. Dogs who make a fuss, who don't wait patiently and virtuously, who don't wag their little tails and perk up their ears. Dogs who cry for help. No one wants them, either.

Last year, when I first started volunteering at the shelter, I tried to steal a dog. He was little, small enough to fit into my backpack. He was ugly, and it turns out he was mean, too; he bit a kid, a three-year-old boy. The boy's family was looking to adopt, and they had this ugly little mutt—we called him Fang because of his ridiculous teeth—out in the visiting room. The kid hadn't yanked the dog's tail or anything, he just started petting him, and that stupid dog sank his teeth right into the kid's forearm. Blood and everything, and the kid screaming. It was awful.

Fang had already been at the shelter for too long, and he was ugly, and now he was a biter. He was a goner. In the chaos, no one really paid me any attention, they just left me with Fang who was now weirdly calm and was looking at me like, "What next?"—like he knew I would understand why he did it. And I did. So while the parents were fussing over the kid somewhere and the shelter manager ran to get the paperwork to document the whole mess, I put Fang into my backpack instead of taking him back to Isolation like I was supposed to.

Of course I got caught. They made me hand over the backpack, dog and all, to another volunteer who took him where I was supposed to take him. I got off with a warning and was told that if I ever tried that again, I'd be banned from volunteering.

The next week, when I went back, Fang was gone.

Not good gone. Not adopted gone.

Dead gone.

《《《

Seth and I met in fifth grade, but he didn't love me until last summer. Even now, I am aware that his love for me is conditional.

Condition 1: Sex. It sounds cliché, and maybe it is, but I am aware of how important sex is in our relationship. It's okay with me; I love it. I love to be with Seth. It didn't hurt, much, the first time, and it's gotten better since then.

Some of my friends have a miserable time trying to find a place and a time when they can be alone together, when they can do the things that I do with Seth, but it's not a problem for us. My dad is practically never home, and my mom sticks to a regular schedule. She plays tennis three afternoons a week with some of her girlfriends, and she never leaves the club until after dark.

Seth's house is more fun than mine, the way it's always crowded with his brothers and all their friends. Seth is the second of four boys. His older brother Wade graduated two years ago, but still lives at home. He spends most of his time in the garage working on his dirt bike. Seth's two younger brothers are like wild animals; they're always together, wrestling and punching each other and calling each other "asshole." They're ten months apart, Seth told me, so they're what people call Irish twins. They're even in the same grade—seventh—because the older one, Anthony, is dyslexic or something and had to repeat kindergarten. He and the youngest, Jude, are exactly the same height. They have a band of miscreant friends that follows after them like apostles, laughing at their jokes and spilling cheese puffs and potato chips on the carpet.

The place is a mess because their mom works and they don't have a housekeeper. Our Shady Canyon development is one of the most expensive in Irvine; Seth's family lives in the Woodbridge development. Older houses, smaller yards. Seth says it's a relief to come over to my place, where everything is quiet and spread out and we can do whatever we want, but I don't know. His place is smaller and messier, and way more crowded, but those all feel like good things to me.

Condition 2: I don't call him. Now, this might sound sort of crazy—not to be able to call your boyfriend—but it's not like that. I mean, it's not like he's ever *said* not to call him. I used to call him, at first, but it didn't take too many times before I figured out that the Seth who called *me* was way more fun than the Seth I called.

It's something about the chase, I guess. He likes it even better when I don't answer the first few times he calls, when I make him wait and guess and worry. Then, when I finally *do* answer, he feels like he's won or something. It's like, I'm not supposed to show how crazy I am about him. Like my real feelings would be too big, or too gross. Instead, I stand just over *here*, an arm's reach away, and I tilt my face just up like *that*, so I'm looking off in a different direction. And I'm so distracted by *whatever* that I can't even be bothered to notice when my phone is ringing or when it buzzes with a text, until finally, at last, I respond. That's when he wants me the most. That's how he likes me. Removed.

Condition 3: We never talk about Apollonia Corado.

Apollonia was new last year, and she's from Portugal, so she's exciting and other and beautiful in a non-Irvine way. Irvine is full of white girls and Asian girls and some Persian girls and not much else. Apollonia drips honeyed foreign appeal.

But we never talk about Apollonia and what happened last winter.

«««

It was in August, two weeks before the beginning of junior year, when Seth called me. It had been a long summer, hotter than usual, and lonely. Louise had been around until the beginning of August, but since then she'd been away with her family in the mountains somewhere, so except for my shifts at the shelter, I was alone. I was lying out by the pool in the backyard, glasses off, trying to keep my body parts from touching each other so that I could tan more evenly. I didn't look at the name before I answered.

"Nina," he said, and I knew instantly who he was, even though he had never called me before. And I knew too why he was calling. I don't know how I knew. Maybe it was the way he said my name, like he was smiling.

He came over that afternoon, and we sat in the hot tub and drank sodas and he did tricks off the diving board to make me laugh. Without my glasses, everything was blurry and perfect, like a fantasy dream. We floated in the deep end of the pool and he kissed me. Our first kiss—with chlorine on our lips and barely any clothes between us. Part of me could barely move my lips to kiss him back, so desperately did I want to freeze that moment. Another part wanted to take his lower lip between my teeth and bite until he bled, just to see if he would stay.

We had those two weeks of summer together, Seth and I. He came to my house and sometimes I went to his and we went to the beach and the movies.

The last night of summer vacation, we did it for the first time. We had almost done it the day before, in my bedroom. I laid a towel on my sheet in case I bled, and then I watched Seth roll the condom over his penis, and I rested my head on my pillow and watched his hands push into the flesh of my thighs, spreading them apart, and I watched him maneuver his latex-wrapped erection, as he pushed and tried to get inside.

I tried to relax, I tried to let him in, I wanted to let him in, but I just couldn't. And Seth was sweet and said it was okay, we'd try again, and then I went down on him instead.

But the next night, the last night of summer, we had dinner at his place with his whole family. There was a big bowl of spaghetti in the center of the table and everyone took turns shaking out Parmesan cheese from the green canister. It was loud and crowded and steamy from the pasta. Anthony and Jude had a friend over, a kid they called Elbows, and even Wade had come out of the garage to eat with us. Their mom looked tired but happy, and it was really nice.

After dinner, his mom—who told me to call her Carol, not Mrs. Barton—offered to take us all out for ice cream to celebrate back to school.

She looked disappointed when Seth said, "Nina and I'll do the dishes." Actually, the look was more than disappointed. She held Seth's gaze until he finally looked away. Then she sighed a little. I guess she thought it would be nice, all her boys together like that, at an ice cream parlor, maybe like they used to do when they were little. But I didn't spend a lot of time feeling bad about it, because as soon as the door shut behind them, Seth grinned at me and asked, "Wanna try again?"

This time, in Seth's room, we didn't bother with a towel.

Seth pushed down my cutoffs and bikini bottoms and went down to the ground with them, looking up at me as he pressed his tongue to my skin.

My legs were shaking, so I sat down on the edge of his bed, and my legs fell open to make room for his mouth. He licked and licked like a cat at a bowl of cream, and when the inside of me felt as wet as the outside, we tried again.

This time, Seth touched my face and looked into my eyes as he fit his penis up against me, as he pushed inside.

The next day at school, there was Apollonia Corado again, her cheeks dark red with shyness, her gaze cast down, a bow in her hair like a child.

Jesus. I hate her.

«««

School goes like this:

The day begins with zero-period AP Chemistry. I don't like chemistry. But I got in to the AP class, and you don't just not do an AP class because you hate the subject. Most of my other classes are AP, too, and the best thing about that is that it means that Seth is in them with me.

Lunch means either going off campus with Seth or pretending not to care if he says he can't. The day begins and ends with Seth. If his Acura isn't in the lot when I pull in, the breath in my chest can't release until I see him in class.

I know it isn't okay to care this much about a boy. I know it's not feminist, or whatever, to make all my decisions based on what Seth would think. I know I'm pitiful. If Seth wants to hang out on a Tuesday afternoon, I call in sick to the shelter. If Seth wants to have sex and I'm on my period, I'm the one to suggest that I give him head. If Seth's energy is off—if he's tense or angry or distant—it's like the molecular makeup of my skin shifts along with it, growing tight and prickly and uncomfortable. I'm a glove that warms to the touch. I'm a sheath that responds to what's inside of me. I'm a chameleon, an octopus, a cuttlefish, and Seth is my only environmental variable.

After lunch is AP Literature with Mr. Whitbey. I guess if I had to choose, English would be my favorite subject. And not just because Seth is in it and Apollonia isn't, but because I like writing the essays. You can say whatever you want in an essay, as long as you defend it. There's no right or wrong—there's just *why*.

When the last bell rings, I get what I need from my locker as fast as I can so that I can be out in the parking lot before Seth gets there. I will arrange my expression into casual disinterest and wait for him to come to me.

My school day is completely average and unremarkable, save for the presence of Seth. Not worth talking about. But it is because of Seth that there are these moments. Little glimpses into something vast and unknowable.

Like when Seth gave me that sideways smile as he held open the door for me last Friday. Tuesday, when I pulled out my ATM card to pay for my lunch at Spinelli's and Seth waved it away, passing his to the waitress instead, pinched like a cigarette between his index and middle finger. When Seth laughed just loudly enough for me to hear during American Lit class, when Whitbey, who everyone knows is gay even though he talks about his "spouse" instead of saying "husband," performed a dramatic reading of "The Bells," that poem by Edgar Allan Poe, and when he said the line, "To the moaning and the groaning of the bells," I whispered, "Balls."

I know it's not cool to define yourself by a boy. Girls are supposed to be independent, these days. We should be Strong Female Characters, we should be tough and self-motivated and grrrrrls instead of girls. We're supposed to run the world—girls—and look unapologetically into the camera. We don't have to smile. We can cross our arms or curl our hands into fists. Except that while we're being tough and independent, we really should be beautiful, too; we're just not supposed to notice, or to care. It's more attractive not to care if you're attractive. That's the idea. I know what I'm supposed to be, and who I'm supposed to be with Seth, but my desire for him overwhelms me at every turn, it fills my throat like an awful tumor, and I am powerless to define myself any other way.

It's his smell, and his eyes, and the way he cuts his nails straight across. It's the way he looks just after he's come, his face softened and sweeter than normal. It's the way his fingers look glazed like a donut after they have been inside of me. It's everything. He is everything.

Last night I dreamed that our house was made of birds. The walls were feather coated, expanding and contracting as the millions of birds that comprised them breathed in and out, in and out. Our staircase was the long curved neck of a giant flamingo, its body curled at the bottom, holding perfectly still to accommodate my weight as I made my way downstairs. There were no windows—only eyes, many eyes, blinking black bird eyes, staring at me as I walked through the great room. The floor was feather coated too, but then it changed its mind in the way dreams do, and instead of feathers I was walking barefoot on tiny sharp beaks, their curved and pointed edges digging into my heels, the pads of my feet, my toes, and then they started to squawk, to cheep, to scream, and the beaks opened and closed and bit my flesh, and dry black bird tongues licked me, and I tried to run but fell instead, and the eyes and the beaks and the feathers consumed me.

"I bought you a present," Seth tells me, Monday after
school. We're standing by the trunk of his Acura, me backed
up against it, him, legs wide, imprisoning me there. His hands
rest on my hips.

"You did?" I am cautious. It's our anniversary—three
months—but I don't expect him to remember it. Men don't
remember anniversaries, and that's okay, my mother has told
me, because then, when they do eventually remember—when
it's too late—then, the gifts are better.

"'Course. It's our anniversary, isn't it? I'm not a total
douche," Seth says, and he kisses me. "Two months, right?"

I feel my face react to his mistake—my forehead clenching
into tight ugly lines, my lips hardening—and he laughs. "You're
so easy," he says. "I know it's three months."

Then he reaches into his pocket, and I think he's going to
pull out a box, a little jewelry box, blue velvet, just the size for
a ring—not an engagement ring, of course, because that would
be ridiculous, but maybe a promise ring, or just a ring, any ring
at all.

Instead, he fishes out his keys and pulls me off the trunk,
popping it open with a push of the remote.

There's a box in there, too big for jewelry. No wrapping

paper, just a plastic bag tied around it. A shoebox, maybe? But he's never asked me what size I wear.

"Thanks." I pull loose the bag ties.

"Don't take it out of the bag," Seth says.

So I don't. I just peek inside.

Not shoes. There's a picture on the box, of what must be inside—a red rubber-knobbed device with a long, black handle. *Three Speeds*, the box announces. And, across the top, *Personal Massager.*

"Thanks?" It comes out kind of like a question, because I don't understand why Seth would give me a back massager. It's not like I've ever complained of back pain.

He grins. "You don't get it, do you?"

"I guess not."

"It's a vibrator," he says.

Then I *do* get it, and I feel melted by the shame.

"It's no big deal," he says. "Wade says it's hard for some girls to come without some . . . help."

Don't cry. Don't cry. "I don't need one of these," I say, and I hate my voice, the wobble in it, I hate that Seth has maybe talked to his brother about *me*, said to him, *"So you know the girl I'm dating, Nina? She's pretty cool. But no matter how much we do it, or how long I lick her, she just can't come."*

"It's no big deal," Seth says again, but of course it's a big deal. It's been three months, and I still haven't had an orgasm. And now he's tired of trying, so he's giving me this *thing*, and I don't want it.

But giving it back to him seems like a bigger deal than just taking it, so I swing my backpack over my shoulder and zip it open, shove the box inside. "Thanks," I say, my eyes focused on the teeth of the zipper as they meet and clench.

My mom wasn't supposed to be able to have kids at all. There's something wrong with her cervix. She found out when she and Dad had been married for a couple of years, after her second miscarriage. She doesn't talk about it much, but I guess there was a miscarriage every year or so, before me and then again after. If each of her miscarriages were an egg, Mom would have enough to fill a cardboard carton. She could draw little faces on them and keep them in the refrigerator.

I was born ridiculously early, at like twenty-seven weeks, and they had to leave me in the ICU for a couple of months before I could come home.

In other words, I was just barely not a miscarriage myself. I wasn't breathing when I came out, I didn't cry, and my veins showed right through my skin. I looked, Mom said, more galline than human. Like a balut, she said. I looked it up, and galline, too. "Galline" means "chicken-like," and a balut, gross as this sounds, is actually a delicacy in some parts of the world. It's a chicken embryo, boiled in its shell.

They worked on me and got me breathing, they made me cry, made me suck, kept me warm in a heated plastic box. Eventually my parents brought me home.

Apparently I wasn't enough, even though I was the egg that hatched, even after everything I had to go through to metamorphose from miscarriage to balut to flesh-and-blood, breathing, eating, bowel-moving human child. Because she kept trying for another. Because that squat crystal glass kept reappearing and disappearing, like a waning and waxing moon.

When I get home from school, I take Seth's present out of my backpack and push it, still wrapped in the plastic bag, onto my closet's highest shelf, cramming it behind my old teddy bears and dolls. I slam the closet door so hard that I rip one of my nails, the one on the ring finger of my right hand. It stings, and my eyes fill with tears, and I slide to the thick, soft carpet and chew away at what's left of the nail, sucking on my fingertip to take away the pain, almost glad for the metallic taste of my own blood.

The house is empty. My parents aren't here. I don't want to be here, either. Apparently no one in my family ever wants to be here, which is pretty ridiculous considering what a nice house it is.

Even if they were here, I wouldn't tell either of them that I was upset with Seth. They vaguely know that we're dating, but they never ask for details and I never offer.

I consider calling Louise to see if she wants to hang out. She used to be my closest friend, until Seth finally noticed me. She had a thing for him, too, but that was okay, back then. We could yearn for him together. We could drive by his house, late at night when we had sleepovers, slowing down as we passed and craning our necks to see if the window that must be his window—the one above the garage—was lit up, wondering, if it was, if that meant he was home, guessing together about what he might be doing—homework, or playing a video game, or taking a shower . . .

She even stuck around after the mess last year, after what I did to Apollonia. She didn't have to, I know that. I wondered then, if the roles were reversed, would I have done the same?

But it changed when Seth picked me. Because then it got weird to hang out with a girl who I knew had a picture of my boyfriend as her screensaver. And it had to be weird for her, too. How could she stand it? I figured I was doing her a favor when I got too busy to hang out with her, when all my free time became Seth time.

But sometimes—like now, or when Seth is busy with something else—I find myself missing Louise. I don't want to just call her up, though, when I have nothing else to do, but I guess sometimes we do things we're not proud of.

The phone rings three times before she answers. "Nina," she says, "Hey."

"Hey," I say. "What are you up to?"

"Nothing," she says. "Homework."

"Do you want to do something?"

"Sure. Do you want to go to the Lab?"

The Lab "Anti-Mall" is this outdoor shopping center filled with bohemian-chic dress shops and cafes and a running store and two hair salons and an Urban Outfitters. It's a mall. Nothing "anti" about it, except the name.

"Okay," I say.

"Can you pick me up?"

"Can't you meet me there?"

"My mom took the car," she says.

I shouldn't have called, but I can't not pick her up now, not when I've been such a dick about avoiding her, even though her house is ten minutes in the wrong direction. "Okay. I'll be there in a few."

I drop my phone on the carpet where it lands with a whispered thud. I close my eyes and rake my fingers through my hair. I take deep breaths.

I don't cry.

Then I relace the boots I've kicked off. Slowly, carefully, I wind each lace around the hooks. I make two bunny ears out of the laces and loop them together into a bow. I pull each knot tight. I slip my phone into the back pocket of my jeans.

My keys aren't where I usually leave them, in the little pewter bowl on my dresser, so I trace my steps downstairs and I find them in a pocket of the jacket I'd shrugged off and thrown into a kitchen chair.

I take the jacket. I lock the house. I walk to my car and slide inside.

Louise is waiting out front when I pull up, so at least there's that. She waves her funny little quick wave and slips into the passenger seat as if no time has passed since the last time we hung out together. As if nothing has changed.

If Louise were a dog at the pound, she'd have nothing to worry about. She'd find a home, no problem.

"Can you believe it's already November?" she says, propping her feet up onto the dashboard, which is annoying, but I don't say anything. "How is that even *possible*?"

"It's crazy," I say. "And that proposal for Whitbey's project is due next week." I find myself loosening up, relaxing, and I wonder what I was so uptight about.

《《《

The anti-mall is crowded, but kind of festive. Even though it's not even Thanksgiving, the stores are decorating for Christmas already. Santa's workshop is being constructed right where it goes up every year, in front of Urban Outfitters, and there's a little wooden sign that reads *Ho Ho Ho! Santa's coming to town on Black Friday!*, which Louise moans and groans over, saying, "Don't they even *see* the irony?"

I don't think she's using the word "irony" exactly right, but I don't give her a hard time about it. We wander into Lavish, this slutty little dress shop where half the girls in our class go to buy dresses for the semiformal dances, and Louise raises her eyebrow and says, "Want to?"

I laugh and say, "Why not?" and then it's on. We both still remember the rules—the left half of the store, from the entrance all the way to the dressing rooms in the back, is mine, and the right half is hers. We go our separate ways just inside the door, and the hunt begins.

Simple rules. Three dresses for each of us. Ten minutes to find them. Then, to the dressing rooms. Sluttiest dress wins.

My first choice is a short red sequined tank dress. It's probably not short *enough* for a win. I could tuck up the hem a few inches, but technically that's cheating. Still, there's a deep V in the front, and the back dips down pretty low, too, so that's good.

Other than us and the sales girl, the shop is empty. Homecoming happened a month ago and winter formal is still two months away, so demand is low right now for sequins and lace.

Next I find an LBD, classic and sexy. I grab one that's a size too small because it's made of a stretchy material that should earn me bonus points. The third is a no-brainer, a hot pink slip dress, ankle length but slit all the way up to the thigh.

Boom. Eight minutes, fifty-two seconds.

Louise barely makes it to the dressing rooms in time.

I pull out to an early lead with the sequined dress; the V-neck, when I yank down on the neckline, descends halfway to my belly button, an easy victory over Louise's cream-colored satin choice.

"I thought it would be more see-through," she groans before retreating back into her dressing room for Round Two.

But my early lead collapses under the divine weight of Louise's boobs. They're an unfair advantage, and I think they've gotten even bigger since last time we played this game over the summer. I don't ask, though, because I don't want to remind her how long it's been since we've hung out.

"Are you girls planning to *buy* any of those dresses?" asks the sales girl as we're heading back into our dressing rooms after Round Three. She calls us "girls" even though she's probably five years older than us. Louise blushes, heat spreading from her miraculous boobs up to her face.

I say, "We were thinking about it, but I don't think they'd pass dress code." I stick my leg out through the dress's high slit. The silky material parts around my thigh like water. The sales girl rolls her eyes all emo and huffs away.

"To the victor goes the spoils!" cheers Louise, fist-pumping wildly, her right boob just barely encapsulated by the silvery rhinestone-laden bodice of her dress. So after we ditch the dresses, avoiding the salesgirl's glare as we pass the cash register without making a purchase, it's off to the Gypsy Den Café where I buy Louise whatever complicatedly named beverage her heart desires, per tradition.

We wander, Louise sucking back her drink, which is practically a milkshake, me taking little sips of my peppermint tea, mostly just peering through windows. It actually feels kind of nice to hang out with Louise again. I try to remember why, exactly, I stopped calling her.

"So," Louise asks as we peer through the window of the haberdashery—this overpriced men's boutique full of hats and cuff links and pocket squares—"How are things with Seth?"

Aaaaand, there it is. That's why. I can hear it in the casual-cool tone, see it in the side glance.

"Great." I take the last sip of my tea and toss the cup into a trash can.

"You guys have been together for a while," she says. "Like three months?"

Is it creepy that she knows how long Seth and I have been together? "Today's our anniversary, actually," I say, remembering Seth's gift and pressing hard on the nail I peeled back, pushing until it hurts again.

Louise laughs. "And you're here with *me*?"

There's this test a feminist made up—the Bechdel test—to determine if a movie is worth seeing. To pass, the movie has to have at least two women in it, and the women have to talk to each other, and they have to talk about something other than a guy.

My entire friendship with Louise would fail the Bechdel test.

«««

"You sure you don't want to come in?" Louise asks as we pull up in front of her house.

"I'd better get home," I say. "That Whitbey proposal."

"Yeah," she says. "Okay." But she doesn't get out of the car. She just sits there in the passenger seat, not even unfastening her seat belt.

"Well, thanks for hanging out," I say after a while.

"Yeah," Louise says. "Thanks for driving." She presses the button to release her seat belt and unlatches the door. "Well," she says. "See you."

I watch her walk up the path to her door. Part of me wants to roll down the window and call to her to wait. She looks lonely. Her *back* looks lonely, if that's possible. Just the way it curls forward at the shoulders. The tilt of her head.

But I don't roll down the window, or call to her, or go inside. Instead I check my rearview mirror the way they taught us in Driver's Ed, and I pull away from the curb, and I drive away.

Condition 2: I don't call Seth. But this time, I do. I put him on speakerphone, so I can drive and talk at the same time, and I push aside the clammy sensation of sickness I feel about breaking this unspoken rule. When he answers, I make my voice playful. "So I didn't get a chance to give you *your* anniversary present."

"Oh, yeah?" He's distracted. I hear a video game in the background, explosions and shouts. I picture him, game controller in his hands, his phone wedged between his shoulder and his cheek.

Right now, I have less than half of him. I want more. So I say, "It's been a week since I started the Pill." Actually it's been six days. Close enough.

The background noise cuts off, and the scratchy connection is suddenly clear. He's holding his phone now. His attention is all on me. "Are your parents home?"

"They're going out tonight," I tell him. "Around six."

"I'll be there at six-thirty," he says.

And he is. Exactly at six-thirty the doorbell rings. I come down the staircase, my hand tracing the long curved line of the wooden banister, dressed in my one purchase from this afternoon—a light pink bra and matching thong. When I open the door to him, Seth's eyes widen with surprise, something that I haven't often seen, and then he smiles.

He snatches me up like a cellophane-wrapped candy and kisses me on the mouth. His arms circle around me and I want to be devoured, I want to be sweet for him and melt on his tongue. I hop up and wrap my legs around his waist, feel already

33

his satisfying hardness. We go like that up the stairs, all sixteen of them, with me in Seth's arms, my tongue in his mouth.

In my room I've lit candles, which Seth doesn't mention, and when he throws me onto the bed, the one on the nightstand flickers out. He shrugs out of his sweater, pulls his T-shirt over his head and tosses it aside, then kicks out of his shoes and yanks down his jeans and his underwear in one fierce movement. Then he's there, naked, the thick horn of him wet-tipped and hard, and a rush of wetness floods the cotton lining of my thong.

"Take off your bra."

I feel, thrillingly, like I'm in a movie, like I'm on display for a vast and important audience, like the whole world is watching as I reach behind my back and unhook the strap. My bra falls into my lap and I push my chest forward, pretending that I think my pointed little breasts are beautiful.

Seth thrusts forward onto the bed and between my legs and against the thin lace barrier that separates us. The hard nose of my teddy bear pokes against my back and I twist to reach it, grab it by an arm or a leg, and toss it to the ground.

My thong gets twisted as Seth takes it off, and I hear it rip when he grows impatient and yanks too hard. I shouldn't care but I do, because the thong is brand new and it matches the bra, and lace can't be sewn back together. But I don't say anything, and then Seth rises above me like a wave and smiles, and I smile back and then he pushes into me, hard and fast and it hurts and feels good all mixed together.

He puts one hand on my stomach to hold me still—he likes it best, he says, when I don't move a lot, when I let him be in charge, and I know too that he likes to feel himself inside of me, under his hand, the back and forth motion of it.

It's clear from his face when he's close, and I brace myself for a second, for the way he usually pulls out roughly right at the end, but then he looks into my eyes and grins, asks, "Okay?"

"Okay," I answer, and then his eyes close and his mouth twists and a vein on his forehead bulges out and he thrusts again and again hard into the center of me and I want to like it but I sort of don't, and I feel him spasm, and spasm, and he makes a sound that would be funny in different circumstances before he is still.

"Fuck," he says, collapsing against me. I run my fingers up and down his spine, feel a few bumps back there, new ones. He hates that he has acne on his back—bacne, he calls it—so I move my hand away to not draw attention to it. Soft now, his penis shrinks inside me and then slips out.

When I get up to go to the bathroom, a runny path of semen, like egg whites, trails down my leg. I am horrified. It feels like I've just peed myself. I don't know what I expected. I guess I thought it would just sort of absorb inside me, or really, I guess I never thought about what would happen at all. The other times when we didn't use a condom, Seth would pull out and come on my stomach or—those two times—on my back. And then he'd use his T-shirt or a sock to wipe me off. But this time, as I walk to the bathroom connected to my room, the sticky wetness drips down my thigh, a couple of drops falling silently to the carpet.

《《《

It's not that I don't have orgasms. It's just that I don't have orgasms with Seth.

He doesn't know this because I haven't told him. Why would I? It would just make him feel bad. And it's not his fault that I don't have orgasms when we're together. And I don't need the stupid vibrator, either. Part of me wants to yell at him, *What kind of a present is* that?

But I don't yell, and I don't tell Seth about the orgasms I do have, that I've been having since I was fourteen years old, all by myself in all kinds of ways—with my hand, with the sharp spray of water from the showerhead, with a pillow, under the covers and between my legs.

And maybe none of these counts. Maybe they're not "real" orgasms, since they're always when I'm alone. It's like that question: if a tree falls in the woods and no one hears it, does it make a sound? Probably solo orgasms don't count if a boy isn't there to witness them. To cause them.

In English class, we're reading *One Hundred Years of Solitude* by Gabriel García Márquez and learning about Magic Realism. This is how Mr. Whitbey defines Magic Realism: making the ordinary extraordinary.

We read the part about José Arcadio Buendía seeing ice for the first time. The author describes it as "an enormous, transparent block with infinite internal needles in which the light of the sunset was broken up into colored stars." When his son touches the ice, he pulls his hand away immediately, exclaiming, "It's boiling."

José Arcadio Buendía calls the ice a miracle. And, to someone without refrigeration who lived in a place where water was never cold enough to freeze, ice would be a miracle, I guess.

"You see," Mr. Whitbey says, leaning against his desk in the way that makes his hips look wide and womanish, "to the modern reader, ice is an invisible convenience. We take it for granted. It's everyday. It's boring. But when we see ice through the eyes of José Arcadio Buendía—" (he breaks into full-on accent to pronounce the name, the way he did last year when we read Gustave Flaubert's *Madame Bovary*)—"then, we see it as magical. Miraculous."

This reminds me of something else, but I can't quite pull it up to the surface. I can feel it itching at me, the connection, and I almost have it, but then my phone vibrates in my pocket and whatever it was—whatever I almost thought of—slips away.

It's a text from Seth. I see him, just a row away, his phone in his hands under his desk, eyes downcast, a little smile that I know is for me even though he's not looking in my direction.

Saturday, the text reads. *You're busy all day.*

I'm supposed 2 hang out w/Louise, I text back, which is not true at all. But I know Seth. I know what gives things value.

Like at the shelter—if two people are considering adopting the same dog, that dog becomes precious. Suddenly, they both *must* have the dog, even if moments before they were on the fence.

Seth's reply is immediate. *Cancel.*

I make him wait a few beats before I reply—*K.*

And then I remember what Mr. Whitbey's lecture about magical ice reminds me of. It's the statue—the first one my mother and I visited in Rome when I was fourteen. The Ecstasy of Saint Teresa.

《《《《

A couple of days later, Thursday after school, I drive straight to the shelter. When I was ordered to find a place to volunteer (can one be ordered to volunteer? Is it still volunteering, then?),

I knew immediately that I'd rather work at an animal shelter than an old folks' home or a food bank, but then I had to choose between the shelter closest to our house—the one that's taken care of by retirees and widows with nothing better to do with their time than give blowouts to bichon frisés and teach labra-doodles how to play fetch, where the shelter's "holding areas" are built in a crescent around a central lawn, a fountain in the middle, donated by some rich cat lady who died a dozen years ago—or the one in Santa Ana.

It used to be that my mother had to drive me, which she resented terribly. "It's bad enough that you did such a stupid thing to that poor girl," she said, "but I don't see why I should be punished for it, too." I never responded. I just stared out my window as we left the groomed, curved streets of Irvine, as we looped onto the freeway, as other cars with other people slid silently by, each car a separate pod of life, each person distinct and someone I would never know.

Since getting my own license and my own car—my mom's hand-me-down Prius, really a gift from my mother to herself, as she didn't have to drive me anymore—I take myself to the shelter. It takes me thirty minutes to get to Santa Ana. I could be there in twenty, but like usual, I stay off the freeway. Here, the shelter is housed in the basement of a concrete-block build-ing in the middle of downtown. Here, the cars don't sparkle, and they're more likely to have bumpers and headlights duct-taped into place than they are to have valid registration stick-ers. In this town, there are bigger problems than pets in need of "rehoming."

Just a few blocks away from the shelter is Santa Ana's newly rehabilitated Arts District. There, young, tattooed artists and writers sip cappuccinos and craft beers at sidewalk cafes; there, local bands unload their equipment on the weekend and set up for gigs in restaurants and art galleries. I know that part of Santa Ana exists, because I've driven up and down its streets. But this building—the shelter—is the only reason I leave Irvine.

I press the lock button on my keychain fob a few extra times for good measure before heading inside.

The sound of barking and the stench of urine hit me at the same time as I pull open the glass door that leads into the reception area. They go together, that sound and that smell.

"Hey, Neen," says Bekah from behind the counter. She barely looks up from her phone.

"Hey," I say. Bekah's wearing the purple polyester vest that marks her as a small-animal volunteer, which reminds me to pull my own ugly vest—green for dogs—out of my backpack and shrug into it. When I first started working at the shelter, Bekah was the person to show me around. She never asked me why I had become a volunteer, which I appreciated, but it meant that I never asked her, either, and I still have no idea what she's doing here. She doesn't look like the kind of person who would want to spend her time in a loud, stinky underground animal jail. I guess I don't either, but she looks interesting and fun, and like someone who must have better things to do. Still, here she is.

"Who's on duty?"

"Ruth," she answers. Ruth is the meanest and the best supervisor at the shelter. She's about sixty-five, built like a pit bull, short and muscly with close-cropped dull gray hair, and as far as any of us can tell she doesn't give a shit about any human being, living or dead. She's all animals, all the time.

"Okay," I say. "See you." I stash my backpack in one of the volunteer lockers and sign in on the computer, reaching over

Bekah to get to the keyboard. She's texting a row of hearts and bows and arrows to her boyfriend Jayson.

Right above her text is a picture. There's skin, and hair, and a silver metal ring with a ball on it. Bekah looks up and catches me staring at the picture. I try to shift my gaze away like I wasn't being a creep, but she just laughs.

"Sorry," I begin, and I start to say more, about not meaning to snoop, but then the door swings open again and there's a young couple with a white-and-black pit bull. The dog's wide mouth is open, his tongue hanging out, and it looks like he's smiling. The couple, though, is not. The girl—twenty, maybe, white with dark purple hair—has the hood of her sweatshirt up, and her face is blotchy and swollen from crying. The guy she's with looks maybe five years older; he's Hispanic and really handsome, and he's the one holding the leash. He's not crying, but he doesn't look happy.

Bekah stashes her phone in the top drawer of the desk. "Did you find a stray?" Her voice is all perky and innocent, even though she totally knows they didn't find a stray. They're here to surrender their pet.

The girl's tears, which were in check, are full-on waterworks now.

"Um, no," says her boyfriend. "We've gotta move, and the new place doesn't take pets."

"Huh," says Bekah. "But this *is* your pet, right?"

"Yeah," he says, scratching the back of his neck. "That's why we're here."

Bekah drops the pretense. "Yellow form," she says, pointing to the plastic rack on the far wall, papered by a rainbow of forms—yellow for voluntary surrender, pink for stray, green for lost pet. Orange for adoption.

The dog flops down and scratches behind its ear—short, pinned ears, sticking straight up, a common pit bull mutilation meant to make them look more menacing, making them practically unadoptable. I look over at the form the guy is filling out. The dog's name is Bronx. Of course it is.

The girl drops to her knees next to the animal and throws her arms around his neck, sobbing into the top of his head. Her boyfriend says, "It's okay, Baby, Bronx is a great dog. He'll definitely get a new home."

He definitely *won't* get a new home. He'll get a couple of weeks to a couple of months in a cage. If he's lucky, a pit bull rescue will pick him up and put him in a foster-home situation for a while, but odds are that he'll be scared and lonely for a few weeks in a cage, getting out for fifteen minutes a day—on walks around the hard-dirt yard with volunteers like me—and then he'll get a needle in his vein and he'll get to be dead.

I know it. Bekah knows it. This guy, from the sideways, tortured glances he throws at his sobbing girlfriend and the dog, knows it. The girlfriend must know it, too—everyone's heard the news about pit bulls, how unadoptable they are. And if Bronx doesn't know it yet, he will soon.

When it comes to dogs, my mom's theory of love is wrong—dogs love their people without conditions, even when their people are total assholes.

I can't stand there anymore, watching this scene. A hard lump fills my throat, tears I won't cry, and I manage to say, "I'll go find Ruth," before I push through the far door into the kennel.

As a teen volunteer, I'm limited as to what I can do, and intake of surrendered pets is beyond the scope of my duties. Which is actually a good thing. If I took Bronx's leash from the girlfriend's hand, I don't know if I could keep myself from telling her what I think of her and her boyfriend and their "move." What I think of people like her, who do what's easy and convenient for them, who throw pets away like paper plates or something.

Ruth is over by the isolation ward where we put the sick dogs in an attempt to keep illness from spreading kennel-wide. Once, a few years ago before I started volunteering, I guess there was this terrible outbreak of canine flu, and two-thirds of the dogs had to be put down all at once. There just wasn't enough funding to medicate that many animals.

Ruth refers to the outbreak as The Auschwitz Incident, even though they didn't gas the dogs. Lethal injection has been the drug of choice at this shelter since 2010.

"Bekah needs you," I tell her. "Surrender."

"Fucking people," says Ruth, which is her mantra.

At this moment, it seems about right. "Fucking people," I say back to her, and she nods.

"The north kennels need to be exercised," she says, before heading up front.

So I head to the north kennels, full of little dogs. A few people wander around, kneeling in front of kennels here and there, where little wet noses press through the chain link, pink tongues curling desperately around outreached fingers. Stanley is sitting where he is always sitting during my shifts—on a bench in the center of the kennels. He's wearing a green vest just like mine and holds a leash across his lap. Then he gets up and walks over to this girl—maybe she's twenty-five or something—who's looking down at a matted white-terrier mix. But he's not great with personal space, and he hovers over her in a way that's kind of creepy. "Do you want to take out the doggy and play with him?" he asks the girl. The dog is doing its best to close the deal, wagging its tail and looking as cute as it can, but Stanley startles the girl, and she stands up suddenly when he talks to her and shakes her head. Probably she was on the fence until Stanley started talking. It's mean to say, because of the way he is, but Stanley's not exactly salesman of the year, if you know what I mean. If Stanley were on the other side of the kennel door, he would have been put down a long time ago. That's all I'm saying. It's not Stanley's fault, and it's not nice. But it's true.

"Hey, Stanley, what's up," I say as I head to the far kennel, grabbing a couple of leashes from a hook nearby.

"Hi, Nina," he says, stretching my name like taffy, like he enjoys the taste of it. Ni . . . n . . . a.

I harness and leash the three Chihuahua mixes from Kennel One and let them pull me up the stairs and to the Play Yard. It's depressing that they all know how to get there given how little time they get to spend there.

The Play Yard is a total euphemism for this awful square of chained-off dirt. There's a bench off in a corner where I flop down after unhooking the leashes and watch the dogs do their initial round of the yard, noses down, sniffing the dirt as they trot the perimeter. After they've all finished sniffing and peeing, and after I bag a loose pile of poop that one of them hunches down to release, I pick up two half-skinned tennis balls and toss them for a while. They get fifteen minutes to play. That's all the time they get out of their concrete cells all day long. If they're lucky, they'll get out five times this week.

We need more volunteers, and more funding, and, of course, fewer dogs, but as things stand now this is all we can give them while we wait for their "forever home" to find them, as the chirpiest volunteers like to say.

Happily ever after. That would be grand. More likely, though, is that at least one of these three will never see the outside of this shelter again. If I liked to bet, I'd put my money on the one we call Ginger to make it out of here. She's pretty cute, and docile, and only three years old. The other two, though . . . odds aren't looking so good for them.

First off, they're both black. That's not me being racist, that's just the truth. Black dogs don't get adopted as often, or as quickly, as lighter-colored dogs. Even if they've passed temperament testing with flying colors, even if they manage to avoid kennel cough, even if they're not old or lame. I'm just reporting the facts of the matter.

And these two don't have anything special going for them. They're not teeny-tiny; they're not especially cute; they're kind of yippy and one of them is a leg-humper. People don't like that.

So I'm the key to their freedom, for these fifteen minutes, and I'm their best friend while I'm throwing the ball, but when time's up I'm their jailer again, clipping the faded, worn leashes back onto the harnesses and taking them back downstairs to Kennel One. This time, they don't lead the way.

When I was little, I would beg my father to play with me. I would poke him, I would tickle him, I would cover his eyes with my hands. I would take his cigarettes and hide them. I would turn up the folded-down corners of his books.

I was so hungry, all the time. Always.

I was a mouth, gaping and undone. I was a satchel, pulled apart and waiting to be filled. I was a chasm, a vortex, a winding endless funnel.

I was the emptiness inside of things. I was the negative space.

Fill me, feed me, give me shape.

There is no such thing as unconditional love, as my mother taught me. Or, at least, there is no such thing as a love that lasts forever. Every relationship inevitably ends in one of two ways: a breakup or a death.

It can be between a parent and a child. It can be between lovers, between friends. Even the relationship of a dog and its master ends inevitably in one of these two ways.

Not long ago, I saw a picture of a dog loyally sitting on its owner's grave. That relationship is over, even if the dog doesn't know it yet. More often, the relationship ends with the dog's death, since dogs don't live as long as people. That is the best ending a dog can hope for—to die first. But sometimes, it happens as it has today at the shelter. The worst way for a dog and human relationship to end. Abandonment. A breakup.

But nothing lasts forever, and there are no happy endings.

I am stopped at a red light just where Santa Ana becomes Irvine, near the 55 freeway. I look at the car next to me. An old lady is driving. She's holding the wheel with both hands. Next to her, his head thrown back and his mouth half-open like he's sleeping, is an old man, or maybe a corpse.

Even if the union lasted fifty years, even if a couple's four hands grow mottled by complimentary liver spots, even if their teeth darken to matching shades of yellow like old piano keys, even if the anniversary is celebrated with silver, somebody dies first.

«««

On Saturday morning, Seth picks me up just after seven o'clock. He's already cruised through Starbucks, and I note with surprise that there are two drinks in the cup holders.

"You got me a drink?"

"'Course I did," Seth says, leaning across the stick shift to kiss me. His lips are warm from the coffee. "You must think I'm a total dick."

I fasten my seatbelt and sip the latte through the slit in the plastic lid. It's hot and foamy and vanilla, my favorite. "Thank you," I say.

"No worries." Seth heads toward the freeway. I'm cold, so I hold the cup in both hands. The windshield wipers clear my view every few seconds. It's not raining hard, just a misty drizzle, and the forecast says it should be clear before noon.

"So where are we going?"

"It's called the Bridge to Nowhere." Seth steps hard on the gas when we get to the on-ramp, zipping past cars in the right lane and zigzagging across the four lanes to the carpool lane on the far left. "It's way the hell out past Azusa."

I have never been to Azusa, even though I've lived my whole life in Irvine. Actually, I haven't been many places farther than the twenty-minute driving radius around my house, except for a few weekend trips to San Diego, the week we drove up the coast to San Francisco, and the time my mom took me to Rome. I almost ask where Azusa is, but I don't want Seth to know how stupid I am about geography, so I say nothing and settle into my role as passenger. Seth turns on music, the electric computer crap he likes, and it's nice. Rain spatters the windshields; the wipers clear it away. Again. Again.

There's no traffic, practically, and it feels good to drive together, to be heading out of town. The music is too loud but I leave it alone. It's enough that Seth remembered what kind of coffee I like.

We drive toward the hills. Seth's hand reaches across and rests on my thigh. It's warm like my coffee.

I wish we could drive forever, not because I like driving so much, but because this is perfect, or as close to perfect as I've ever felt—the weight and warmth of Seth's hand. The latte. The forethought and planning that went into today. The sensation of having been chosen, of being wanted. Of being exactly right.

The rain softens and slows until it stops, and a shaft of light pierces through the clouds. It's almost ridiculous how amazing it seems when a rainbow appears right in front of us, framed like a picture in the windshield.

"Look!" I say.

"I fucking hate rainbows."

"No one hates rainbows. They're *rainbows*. They're *amazing*. How can you hate rainbows?" I'm practically sputtering.

"God, Neen, you're so easy," Seth says, and he laughs and squeezes my thigh. "I'm just kidding." His smile is nice.

I lay my hand on top of his hand, and he spreads his fingers so mine can web in between his.

In Azusa, we stop at a drugstore to pick up cold bottles of water. "Maybe go get some sunscreen," he says at the last minute, right before the checker rings us up.

"Back of the store," she says, bored. "By the pharmacy."

"I'll meet you at the car," Seth says.

There are like thirty different kinds of sunscreen. I pick one that says "waterproof" in case it rains again or something. The line up front has grown, so I go to the pharmacy counter to pay.

There's one person ahead of me. She's peeling bills from a roll, counting off fives and ones. "Do you want to talk to the pharmacist?" asks the cashier. He's an old white guy with one of those monstrous guts.

"Okay," says the girl, and she pushes the money toward the register. He takes it and gives her a handful of change and slides a box over to her. Then she steps to the side to wait. I put my sunscreen on the counter, but glance over to look at her purchase.

The box is in front of her. It's violet and white with a green arc over the letters that read *Plan B One-Step*, and beneath, in pink, *Emergency Contraceptive*.

The pharmacist comes over, this completely generic-looking woman who is older than twenty and younger than fifty, lank dark hair pulled back in a ponytail. "You ever used this before?" she asks the girl.

"Seven dollars and sixty-three cents," potbelly guy says to me, and I hold out my ATM card, all my attention on the conversation happening beside me.

"No," the girl whispers.

"Just swipe the card," potbelly guy tells me.

"It's just one pill," the pharmacist says. "You take it by mouth within seventy-two hours of unprotected sex. Has it been less than seventy-two hours?"

"Um," says the girl. "I think so. Yes."

"It's asking for your PIN," the cashier prompts me.

"The sooner you take it after unprotected intercourse, the more effective it is," the pharmacist says. "The pill contains levonorgestrel, the same as what's in birth-control pills. It's just a concentrated version of the same thing. Okay?"

The girl nods. I've keyed in my PIN, and now the cashier is holding out my receipt.

"Will it hurt?"

"Common side effects include nausea, some abdominal pain, fatigue, headaches, and changes in your menstrual cycle. You might be dizzy. If you vomit within two hours of taking the pill, you may need to speak with a doctor about getting another dose."

"Will there be anything else?" The potbellied cashier looks annoyed, even though there's no one in line behind me.

"No," I say. "Thanks." I turn to go and look back to see the girl slipping the box, furtively, into her bag as though she's stealing it, even though I saw her pay for it already.

《《《《

We drive and drive. The road turns to dirt and we drive more. We roll the windows down and breathe in wet-dirt, my favorite smell. How can dirt smell clean? But it does.

Finally we reach the end, where the road widens into a parking lot. It's pretty full but not packed, with cars that belong here—Jeeps and trucks with mud flaps—and cars that don't, like Seth's Acura. Seth loads the water bottles, jerky, and trail mix into his backpack. He kneels to double-knot his laces and grins up at me, a golden wing of hair across his forehead.

He told me as we drove that the hike is over four miles each way. He told me that there really is a bridge to nowhere, it's not a poetic metaphor. "It was built in the thirties," Seth told me. "It was supposed to connect Wrightwood with the San Gabriel mountains, but a flood washed out a big chunk of the road. The project was abandoned, but the bridge was already built."

"So now people hike to it."

"People do all kinds of crazy shit."

The trail we take away from the parking lot is wide. Plumes of dust puff up with each step I take. The trail is crisscrossed with the imprints of people who have walked this way before us: hiking boots with their diamond-patterned treads, the zig-zags of rubber-soled cross trainers, here and there a dog print, some big enough to look like a coyote's.

We walk side by side along the trail as the sun rises up over our heads, growing hotter and brighter as the morning's dampness evaporates, as the trail thins and thins, into the mouth of a canyon. I wish we were holding hands but we're not, and then the trail gets too skinny and we fall into single file, me behind Seth.

We finished our coffee in the car, and even though I'm not thirsty I wish I were still holding the cup.

There's a river that we have to cross several times to stay on the trail. The first two times we have to go across, it's no problem; we make the first pass by hopping from rock to rock, and the second time we cross there's a fallen log that forms a bridge for us. But the deeper into the canyon we hike, the faster the water travels and the deeper the river becomes.

At the third crossing, we have to wade. "Some years this river can get pretty treacherous in the winter," Seth says. He's strung his sneakers around his neck, tied together by the laces, and shoved his socks into the back pocket of his shorts. I chose the wrong shoes—my Tevas, which are good for short walks,

51

but are already rubbing my feet raw. It's been too long since I've been hiking, I guess, and the soles of my feet are tender. I take them off before stepping into the river, and the cold water feels wonderful. I wish I could just stop right there and let the icy water wash over me for the rest of the day.

"How far did you say it is?" I ask.

"Far," Seth answers. He's reached the other side and sits on a rock to put his socks and sneakers back on. "Are you okay?"

"Yeah," I say. "I'm fine." I force myself to walk out of the water. "It's just that my feet are a little sore. I should have worn my tennis shoes or something."

Seth frowns as he looks down at my water-chilled, reddened feet. I feel exposed and stupid. I should have known better than to wear sandals, even hiking sandals.

"Take my socks," he says, pulling them off his feet and holding them out to me. They're black with a red stripe of stitching across the toe.

"No, that's okay."

"You'll never make it to the bridge and back otherwise. Sorry they're kind of sweaty."

I take the socks and sit down next to him. The socks are warm and damp. *He gave me his socks*, I think stupidly. It just feels like this big thing, like it means something that he's willing to be less comfortable so that I will be more comfortable.

Gingerly, I work my left foot into one of the socks. It's too big. The toe part flops loosely past my toes. I refasten my Teva over the sock. It is better this way, with the sock between my foot and the straps.

We hike for two more hours before we make it to the Bridge to Nowhere, and we hear it before we see it—the music, the cheers.

It's been so quiet on the path—just our shoes crunching in the dry leaves, the occasional clatter of a kicked rock, a few other hikers here and there, but all into their own thing—that when I first hear the music, I think it must be coming from Seth's phone.

Then I hear the first cheer. I still can't see the bridge, but the cheer is pretty loud.

"They're jumping today," Seth says, looking back at me and smiling this open happy smile, just so much smile that it kind of shocks me. I hadn't noticed how long it had been since I'd seen Seth smile—really smile, like from joy, not from sarcasm or irony or because he was mocking someone—until this smile broke across his face.

Have I *ever* seen him smile like this?

(Have I ever made him smile like this? Do his after-sex smiles count, the half-lidded eyes, the satisfied grin?)

We turn a bend and there it is—this expanse, this vista, this bizarre unexpected impossible *party*.

There's the bridge, kind of old fashioned, its railings made from concrete pillars, the buttresses holding it up, bleached white like bone from their years out here in the sun. All along the railing on one side of the bridge are people. Mountain bikers in their silly, tight, padded-crotch shorts, hikers dressed in official hiking gear like those ugly UV shirts and pants that zip away at the knee to become shorts, and kids our age or maybe a little older, girls and guys both in cutoffs and hiking boots and tennis shoes, and there's music, the kind of music that you play at a house party, loud and strong and more about the beat of the drum and the scream of the singer than the lyrics. You know what the song's about without knowing the words—it's about anger and freedom and being wild.

All the energy on the bridge is turned inward, toward this black chick dead center, who's looking down at her crotch where this lanky white guy kneels. He's fastening the straps of a harness that she's stepped into, he's checking the buckles and pulling on the end of the strap to make sure it's secure. And then he nods and stands, and she shoulders into the top part of the harness, and he checks the buckles there, too. Then he hands her a helmet that she puts on, pushing down over her tight, dark curls and fastening the chinstrap.

The guy attaches the end of the bungee cord to the front of the harness. He offers her a hand but she doesn't need it, and she scrambles up on the top of the railing like she hasn't ever heard of fear or doubt or regret. There's this one long moment when she stands there, arms outstretched, staring straight ahead, and the whole bridge full of people, me and Seth included, share one held breath.

Then she dives.

The bungee uncoils behind her as she falls, like an umbilical cord, like Rapunzel's braid, and my stomach tightens with the certainty that it won't hold, that it will break and then she will break too on the rocks that jut and crest from the river below, that the fast-moving water will dilute the blood that she will spill, that her skin will crack like an egg that can never be put together again. Yolk and blood and frayed rope. Rocks and water and nothing more.

But the rope is not made of hair. It's not fragile like flesh or human meat. An umbilical cord would burst. Hair would fray. The cord holds. She reaches the end of its length and it stretches farther, its elastic slowing her. The tips of her fingers brush the river. For a fraction of a moment gravity doesn't exist and she hangs upside down, frozen, a statue.

The crowd explodes in a cheer, and I'm yelling, too, all our voices yelling out together as she's yanked hard back toward us. She flips over and flails now, out of control, her hips higher than her arms or legs or head, and she bounces once, twice, three times, and it's a crazy thing to see. It's a crazy thing to *do*, to jump off a bridge, to trust that harness and that cord and that guy, even, that he's not stoned or something, that he's really sure about how perfectly he's latched all the things that need to latch.

She's done bouncing now, she's just kind of swaying there partway down, and they're hauling her back up, and I'm thinking about the bridge, about how she has to trust that, too, not to crack or crumble into dust.

Then she's back on the bridge safe and sound. The same guy undoes the harness and she steps out of it. It's someone else's turn.

Seth and I walk across the bridge and find a patch of shade where we sit down. He pulls a bottle of water out of his pack and takes a long drink before handing it to me, saving the other bottle for our hike out. I take it and put my lips right where his were.

"So, what do you think?" he asks.

I look around at the rocks and the people and the river and the bridge. "It's amazing."

"Would you do it?"

"Jump, you mean?"

He nods.

Would I? I shrug. "Would you?"

"Definitely," he says. He reaches out for the water bottle. When I pass it back, he takes another long drink and I watch the way he tips back his head, the way his lips meet the rim of the bottle, the way his Adam's apple moves up and down as he swallows. The shape of the nail beds on his fingers. The line up his forearm along the edge of his muscle. The darkened pits of his T-shirt, the way the neckline is stretched out. The hair on his legs and his feet in his shoes with no socks.

"I'd do it with you," I say.

He screws the top back on the bottle. He looks at me straight in the eyes. He's thinking something I can't read from his gaze, but it feels really, really important. "Would you?" he asks.

My mouth feels dry even though I just drank water. I nod.

"Okay," he says.

Okay? Okay what?

I clear my throat. "You probably have to be eighteen, right? I mean, they're not going to just let us jump. There's like, liability. We'd need parent waivers or something." I'm backpedaling, and I hate that he can tell.

"Only if we want to use their equipment."

I laugh. "What've you got in that backpack, Seth? I thought you just packed sandwiches."

"Peanut butter and jelly," he says. "And some pistachios."

"So you want to just jump off a bridge? No bungee cord? Funny."

But he's not being funny. He doesn't smile, or look away, or even blink. This feels like a test, and I don't know the answer.

I'm not even sure I really understand the question. Or why he would ask it. He couldn't really be asking me to jump off a bridge with him—to die with him. Is he really asking how much I love him? If my love for him is conditional on staying alive?

"Hey," I say, "Do you want to walk down to the river?"

"What I want," Seth says, "is to jump off the bridge."

56

We don't jump off the bridge. We don't walk down to the river. We eat the sandwiches, we share the pistachios, we watch other people tie in and leap and scream and cheer and the divide between us widens into a chasm.

Then we hike back out.

I answered the question wrong. Following Seth, watching the muscles underneath his T-shirt move as he leads the way, I hate myself. It was a bluff, and I should have played along. I should have said yes, anything, let's go, let's jump, as long as we can hold hands when we go over. I should have said something different. I should have done something different. But now it's too late, and though Seth walks no further from me on the way out than he did on the way in, the distance is impassable.

I follow and I think of a hundred things to say but none of them is the right thing and so I say nothing.

Inside Seth's socks, inside my Tevas, my feet hurt again. I can feel the blisters peeling open, but I don't mind. I put my focus there, on the pain, on the top of my big toes and the backs of my heels and across the balls of my feet, and I make myself feel it all the way through. I don't let myself hobble. Each step, I press first with my heel, then articulate up through the arch of my foot and onto my toes, feeling the sting and burn and rip, and welcoming it.

We're almost back to the car when I can't stand it anymore. I jog-step to catch up with him. I take his hand, and he stops and looks at me. I can't read his face. It's like I forgot how, or maybe I never really knew how to begin with, but I thought I did, but I was wrong.

I pull him off the trail behind some trees, and I push him

57

against a tall rock, and before I can worry if someone will come by and see us I go down on my knees like the guy on the bridge, except instead of tightening a harness I'm unfastening his pants.

I pull him out of his underwear and he's soft in my hand. I don't look up at his face before I open my mouth and pull him into it, and I pull and I suck until he grows hard and he makes sounds that mean he likes it, and I keep going and going and when he says, "I'm going to come," I don't pull away.

The jet of him is warm and salty and tastes like thickened sweat. He breathes hard and his hands are tight fists at his eyes.

There's not much water left in the last bottle but what there is Seth gives to me, and I drink it as he arranges himself back into his shorts. We walk the rest of the way back to the car, still not talking, but at least now side by side on the widening trail.

I carry the empty bottle. We drive home.

《《《《

Yet I, least of all souls
Take Him in my hand
Eat Him and drink Him,
And do with Him what I will!

It's a real thing written by a religious mystic way back in the thirteenth century. She was talking about worshipping Jesus, but come on. She was talking about sex, right? Sex with Jesus?

That was what she wanted—to give Jesus head. And I totally understand it.

When you love someone the way that I love Seth—the way that woman who wrote the poem loved Jesus—you want to serve him. And you want to paralyze him so he can't go away.

Grandparents tell their grandchildren, "I'll eat you up!" It's the same idea, in a weird way. You want to consume the person you love. You want to eat him so he's inside you, so he becomes part of you, so he can't leave you.

Grandparents eating grandchildren. Chewing the flesh and drinking the blood of Jesus every Sunday in church. Swallowing Seth's cum on the trail. Is it different?

Is it?

Once upon a time, a beautiful daughter was born to a king and his wife. At the age of thirteen, she vowed perpetual virginity in the name of her Lord Christ.

But when the Emperor of a nearby land threatened to make war on her father, and when her father took his family with him to Rome to negotiate peace, the daughter Philomena's sacred virginity was threatened.

With one look at Philomena's fair visage, her downcast eyes and lovely lips, the Emperor was struck with desire. "Give me your daughter to be my wife," he demanded. "And I will not wage war on you."

Philomena, who wanted to be of service to her family but had already sworn to be of service only to God, refused.

Where at first the Emperor had felt love, now he felt the strongest of hate for this young woman who dared to defy his wishes, who dared to prefer no husband at all rather than the hand of an Emperor.

And thus began Philomena's torments.

First, the Emperor ordered that she be whipped, and whipped she was, her back stripped bare and a heavy leather strap brought down against its tender flesh, again and again, until the flesh was flayed and bloody, until there was nothing there that could be called a back at all.

But that night, two angels visited her in her cell and with their gentle ministrations, Philomena's flesh ceased to bleed, closed up again, and became as if it had never been touched.

When the Emperor saw this, his malice doubled, and this time he ordered that Philomena be drowned.

Philomena was tied to an anchor and lowered into the river, her long hair floating on the water's surface after the rest of her had been submerged; but the angels returned, and this time they cut the ropes that bound her and took her safely to the riverbank, where she coughed up the river water and lived.

Now the Emperor ordered arrows fired on the source of his aggravation and lust. When the arrows pierced her flesh, wounding Philomena in her legs and arms and chest, the angels came behind and, with a pinch of their fingers, removed the arrows and closed the wounds. When the archers shot again, the angels turned their arrows aside so that Philomena was unharmed by them; and when the archers sought to shoot a third time, the angels caused the archers to fall down dead.

Still the Emperor would not be stopped, not by the miracle of angels, not by anything at all, and he ordered that Philomena be decapitated.

And so she was, her head severed from her body at three o'clock in the afternoon on a Friday, the time of death aligning with the time of the death of her bridegroom Jesus Christ who had preceded her to heaven, and at last Philomena was free to join him, and she lived happily ever after.

He doesn't call and I don't call and I know it's over.
I blame myself, myself, only myself. He put forth a condition;
I failed to meet it. And that is how our story ends.

«««

Apollonia Corado came to our school just after winter break
last year. That's the best time to be a new student—when
everyone is bored of each other, when a new face makes the
most impact.

Louise was assigned to show her around, to make sure she
knew where her locker was and where to eat lunch. And Louise
did a good job, of course, because Louise is a good girl, but also
because there is attention by association and Apollonia Corado
is beautiful.

My mother told me that a man's love for a woman is conditional on her beauty, but what she didn't say is that the love
everyone else has for her (or doesn't) is conditional on that, too.

"There are two girls bathrooms in this wing of the school,"
I heard Louise telling Apollonia as she escorted her through
the hallway before lunch. "But you'll want to use the one down
there, at the end of the hallway, because it has new toilet seats.

The ones in the other bathroom haven't been replaced in years, no one knows why, and they're gross."

That was solid advice; the toilet seats in the other bathroom *were* gross, and over the years girls had carved words into them, words that pressed into the skin of your butt and thighs when you sat down—SLUT and CUNT and WHORE.

Why anyone would make the effort to deface a toilet seat was beyond me, and why no one had replaced them was a mystery, too. Louise and I had a theory that it was because the janitor, a white guy in his fifties whose name tag read ALLAN, which could be a first name or last, believed those words to be the name tags all of us girls should wear, and that we deserved to sit on them when we were peeing.

That first day after winter break, squatted down in front of my locker, half-hidden behind the swung-open metal door of it, I watched the hallway of students and teachers as Apollonia and Louise moved through them.

I watched as Seth walked up to them, the smile he wore saying everything even before he spoke. "If you're done telling her about the toilets, Weez, I can take it from here."

Seth—and most of the boys—called Louise "Weez," a nickname she pretended to hate but really embraced for the simple fact that they'd bothered to give her one at all.

"That's okay," Louise said, clutching her books to her chest. "I'm supposed to show her around. I was assigned."

"I don't think it matters who takes the new girl to the cafeteria," Seth said. "If anyone asks, I'll tell them you had to take a shit and asked me to finish the tour. Come on," he said to Apollonia.

Apollonia smiled at Louise, not unkindly. "Thank you

for your help," she said, and the words from her mouth, with her accent, sounded royal. And then she turned with Seth and walked away.

Louise's shoulders raised and slumped, a motion of hers I recognized well, and then she came over to lean against the lockers next to me.

I closed my locker, spun its dial, and stood. Together we watched them, Seth and Apollonia, as they walked down the hallway, their bodies closer to one another than strictly necessary.

"All these years we've loved him," she said, in her annoying brand of unnecessary honesty, "and on her first day she waltzes in and he's gone."

《《《

They were a matched set, Seth and Apollonia, she the dark-haired pepper to his blond salt. From the moment when Seth replaced Louise as Apollonia's guide, where one of them went, the other followed. And it was Seth following Apollonia as often as it was the other way around. He'd hold her purse while she rifled through her locker; he'd share his tray in the cafeteria, waiting patiently as she picked through the yogurt choices and selected the one she wanted.

It made me angry. Furious. Who was *she* to be waited for? Who was *she* to have her purse held, and her preferences considered? I'd wanted him all these years, and this girl, she'd just arrived. That was all she had to do. Just show up, and he was hers.

That's when I learned that beauty can make people love you, but it can make them hate you just as surely.

It's Sunday night at six o'clock, and I haven't spoken to Seth since he dropped me off twenty-seven hours ago. I don't know where my parents are. They're not home. No one is ever home. It's like a mausoleum, our safe and lovely house, and even when we're here it still feels like no one is, with each of us retreated to separate vaults—me in my room, Dad in his study, Mom in the kitchen or the laundry room or in her bedroom with the door closed. But tonight it doesn't really matter where they are. All my energy is sent out of the house, down the street, and away toward Seth, wherever he might be.

I have no idea why we have this ridiculously huge house. Sometimes I click through pictures on my laptop of the "tiny house" movement, dreaming of having my very own doll-house-proportioned home. The tiny houses are like four hundred square feet—smaller than my bedroom—so everything in them is necessary. There's no room for anything extra, but that's okay, because you have everything you need. You've got a two-burner stove, and a half-sized fridge, and a table with two chairs, and a place to sit and read. You've got a toilet and a shower. Upstairs there's a sleeping loft big enough for a double mattress or maybe a queen if you splurge a little, but not tall enough to stand. And that's okay because the sleeping loft is for sleeping, not standing.

A tiny house is tight and necessary and cozy-warm, womb-like in its intimacy.

Our place is an entombment of waste and space and emptiness. No wonder my mother has lost so many pregnancies; no wonder my own heart feels cold and tight and lonely all the time. These aren't human proportions, the vastness of our entry hall, the echo of our scrubbed-clean kitchen, the vast ceilings and smooth walls and processed air-conditioned air. There's nowhere in our house to grab hold, to take purchase, to nestle and connect and grow. I hate it here, and every time I enter the front door I want to leave.

I try and try, but I can't find him out there. I can't feel him, connected to me. It's a severed cord.

Thinking of the cord that no longer connects us brings back the image of that girl jumping, the stretchy rope that suspended her above the river, tying her to something.

And then I think of another cord, this one attached to a black-handled vibrator, the other end of it red and round and rubbery like an oversized clown nose.

I reach a blind hand up to the top shelf of my closet and I fish around until my fingers find the plastic bag, and I pull on it until Seth's gift falls from the shelf and into my hand.

I sit on the floor near the foot of my bed and open the plastic bag, pull open the cardboard flaps at the top end of the box, and slide out the vibrator.

This is the only present Seth has ever given me. There was the coffee yesterday, and the times he's bought meals for me, and that one time he picked a dandelion from his front yard when he'd walked me to my car.

The meals and drinks I'd chewed and swallowed, I'd digested, I'd turned into pee and shit. The dandelion I'd blown on, sending tiny white buds far and wide, destroying the flower even as I wished upon it that Seth and I would last forever, together.

All I have is this. Plastic and rubber and a long black cord.

I take the cord in my hand and untwist it. I push my thumb against the double-pronged plug until it hurts, and when I take it away there are two indentations in the pad of my thumb, as if I've been bitten.

Then I get up and close my bedroom door. I lock it.

The cord is long enough to stretch from the outlet where my bedside lamp is plugged in to nearly the center of my double bed. I push down my jeans and underwear, step out of them, leave them on the floor.

I sit on the edge of my bed and flick the switch on the side of the vibrator. The sound as much as the movement startles me—it hums loudly, embarrassingly so.

I switch it off. I find my phone and plug it into my stereo and start a song at random. It's not the song that matters—I'm not setting a mood here. It's the noise I need.

It's an old song, recently rereleased—"I Wanna Be Your Dog." I turn up the volume and yank back the covers on my bed, slide beneath them, and don't restart the vibrator until it's muffled underneath the blankets.

Between the closed door and the loud music and the heavy quilt, no one but me could possibly hear the angry buzz of Seth's first and final gift to me. I let my knees splay open and find my slit with my fingers, the soft hooded nub at its apex, and I guide the red rubber ball against it.

My back arches and I hiss in a breath at its first wonderful, terrible contact. A jolt of pleasure shoots through me and I yank the vibrator away before placing it back against me, this time very gently.

It almost hurts, the hum, the buzz, the stroke of it, so different from the jet of warm water that pours from the shower-head, so different from the press of my own hand, so different from the wet lapping of Seth's tongue.

It's remembering Seth's tongue that pushes me into the

first orgasm, the sweet way he'd press it just there, right where I'm holding the rubber tip of the vibrator, the anxious, ineffective, hopeful lapping of his tongue. And I squeeze my eyes shut and my hips buck up against the vibrator, and my neck gets tight and my toes are stuck in a weird curled spasm, and I can't tell and don't care which way is up and which way is down, and the music is playing and I hear the words of the song and picture myself heeled at Seth's side, a faithful pet, a happy dog, an obedient good girl who follows rules and gets rewarded. I'm hearing the buzz of the tool in my hand, and every part of me vibrates in a way that makes me forget my name, and I don't care I don't care I don't care, just as long as this feeling persists, and I'm wound so tight that I might break like a thread, like a cord, like a promise, and then I do break, I break and I shatter and I'm lost in the vibration of my coming, and maybe I make a sound and maybe I bite my lip and my legs spread into butterfly pose and then fold up like wings and I fly, and then I shiver and it's behind me, that pleasure. I'm back in my own flesh and my mouth tastes like blood.

I turn off the vibrator and it lays quiet in my hand.

This is a long song, almost five minutes, but it's not even halfway over and I've already come. I want to unplug the vibrator and put it away. I want to lie perfectly still in this spot for a hundred years. I want to disappear. I want to scream.

I don't do any of these things. Instead I flick the vibrator's switch back on, I grip the black handle tightly, and I press the nose of it against the center of me. The next orgasm hits almost at once, more of a tsunami than a wave, and I'm overcome and lost in it. When the crest of it passes, I don't turn off the vibrator, I don't take it away. I shove it more firmly against me, and I squirm beneath its relentless hum. I force myself to come again and again, until the pleasure morphs into punishment, until I ache, until I lose count of how many times I've come and how many ways I've lost Seth. The orgasms are a seething ocean, each cresting atop the one before, and they drag me back and away, like an undertow.

PART II
EROS AND THANATOS

When I was fourteen, my mother and I traveled together to Italy.

I wasn't supposed to go with her. My father was. They had planned the trip together as a second honeymoon, to celebrate their twentieth wedding anniversary. For months, travel brochures and packing lists had littered the dining room table. Mom had changed her laptop's screensaver to a picture of the Basilica. She got their passports out of the safety deposit box and researched the Euro and compared places to stay and transportation and restaurants. She pulled out her old language books from college and reviewed Italian verb conjugations.

Then, twelve days before they were set to leave, a week before my final days of middle school, I came home to find the dining room table bare again, polished and still as glass.

Mom's car—the Prius I would inherit—was in the drive-way, but the house felt echo-empty. The quiet hum of the air conditioner, the clicking of the clock, and my own breath.

"Mom?" I called. "Hello?"

No answer. I took a soda from the fridge and drank it standing at the counter. Then I pulled open the recycling bin to throw away the can, and there it was—my parents' trip, all of it, the travel brochures and the packing lists and even the passports. In the garbage.

I set the can on the countertop. I looked around, then back down at the pile in the trash. I couldn't leave it there. It was a mistake, it had to be. Maybe there was a new cleaning lady who had thrown it all away by accident.

I pulled it all out of the bin and stacked it neatly on the counter. Then I threw away my can. Then I didn't know what to do.

I stood there at the kitchen counter with one hand on the stack of papers. No cleaning lady would throw away passports. I knew that.

"You're home."

I gulped, startled by my mom's voice, feeling a surge of guilt about the papers, even though I hadn't been the one to throw them away.

"I found these in the trash," I said. "I didn't throw them out."

"Of course you didn't," Mom said. "You wouldn't do that." She took the papers from where they lay and knocked them together against the countertop, even though they were already perfectly straight. Her dark hair fell in waves around her face. Her hair was hardly ever down. And I saw that she wasn't wearing lipstick.

She looked up from the papers and smiled at me. A tired smile, not a real one. "It was stupid of me," she said. "I threw them away. I was just coming down to pull them back out of the trash."

"Oh," I said. "Okay."

She held the stack of papers against her chest. "You can't just throw away a passport," she said, as if I didn't know that, as if I'd been the one to put them in the recycle bin.

"Mom? Are you all right?"

She sighed and went over to sit at the kitchen table. "I'm fine," she said. "Just disappointed. Your dad has to cancel our trip."

"Oh," I said. "Why?"

She looked at me appraisingly for a moment, like she was trying to decide if I could handle the truth. I stood straight and tried to look smart, hoping she'd see something in me that inspired her to confide in me. But she must not have seen what she'd been looking for, because when she answered, it was just one word, and a lie—"Work," she said.

"Oh," I said again, and I turned to leave, tears stinging my eyes.

"Nina," she said. I stopped, but I didn't turn back around. "Do you want to go to Italy?"

《《《《

And that was how I came to find myself missing the final days of middle school, missing the good-bye party and the yearbook signing and the graduation ceremony. "It's just silly anyway, isn't it?" was the way Mom put it, and suddenly it did seem silly, all those things I'd been looking forward to doing. It seemed silly and childish. And it was clear to me that Mom's need to leave for Italy immediately was greater than my desire to do all those silly things. So she changed the name on Dad's reservation to mine, and moved forward our departure date, and within twenty-four hours I was flying across the country and then across the ocean.

It wasn't until three hours into our flight that I realized that I hadn't seen my father before we left, and that I hadn't said good-bye.

Once upon a time there was a beautiful young princess whose parents, though united in marriage, were divided in worship, as her father the king was a worshipper of the old pagan gods and her mother the queen was a Christian. Like her mother, Dymphna followed the teachings of Jesus Christ, and with her womanhood new upon her, she vowed her eternal chastity to her Lord in Heaven.

But shortly after Dymphna's consecration to Christ, her mother died. Though Dymphna found solace in prayer, her father did not. As days turned to weeks, his closest friends and advisors began to worry about his destructive sorrow, and they determined that he should remarry. The king agreed, but only if they could procure for him a bride who might resemble his dear, dead wife.

But none could be found that came close to matching his wife in beauty, such was her distinction. None, that is, but for her daughter, Dymphna, whom her father decided he would take as his bride, as no one else would do.

When Dymphna heard of his terrible plan, she fled from her castle with her confessor, Saint Gerebran. They ran and hid, and when Dymphna felt they were at last far enough away to be safe, she began to dedicate herself to helping the poor in the land where she had taken refuge. All was well for some months until the king found them. Immediately, he ordered that the priest's head be cut off, and so it was.

"Daughter," he spoke, his own sword heavy in his hand, "there is no call for your death this day. Return to me, and become my wife in your mother's stead, and together we can rule."

But Dymphna refused, and as she lifted her chin in defiance, her father spied the long milky path of her neck, and his desire twined tight with his rage, and his sword, which had been limp at his side, rose high and mighty into the air.

And he fell upon his daughter, and his sword impaled her neck, and her head rolled free to where her confessor's rested, her eyes turned heavenward, toward where her soul had gone to live happily ever after.

Rome moved at an entirely different pace than Irvine.
Life in Irvine was all about moderation—the street lights were timed to anticipate traffic flow, keeping drivers from abrupt stops and starts; shops closed early, by nine or ten; regular speed bumps ensured that no one went too fast through residential areas. Moderation.

Rome was all about extremes. People drove too fast, motor scooters edging up on sidewalks and blasting their horns at pedestrians to make them get out of the way. Tourists took too many pictures. Meals started late and went on for hours, the sun setting and the sky darkening before the waiter would bring the check.

"Don't they *want* to get paid?" I asked Mom.

People meandered on street corners, gesturing in big wide arcs with their hands, the ash from their cigarettes threatening to spill. People talked loudly, and laughed loudly, and embraced and kissed in a way that made me feel so boring and ridiculously American.

Mom had first come to Rome during her junior year of college. This was where she and my father had met. That much I knew, but none of the details. It had never occurred to me to ask, I guess.

When we first landed, I stood feeling stupidly half-awake as Mom hailed a taxi. *"Portarci al Boscolo Exedra Roma,"* she told the driver.

"Naturalmente, bella," he answered, smiling warm and slow at us in the backseat. He dropped a heavy wink—at me, at my mother, I couldn't tell—before he turned back around and pulled away from the curb.

The hotel was beautiful, an old castle they'd made into a modern resort, and the people working there were beautiful, too. Our room had only one bed, and as I sat on its edge I thought about how this was supposed to be my parents' romantic getaway. I thought about the things they might have done together in this room, in this bed.

Mom was putting away her dresses in the closet, taking them out of her suitcase one at a time, shaking out the wrinkles, hanging them on wooden hangers just like the ones we had at home.

"Tell me how you met Dad again?"

"Again?" she said. "I don't think I've ever told you before."

"Well, I know you met here, in Rome," I said. "But where, exactly?"

"At a church," she said. "In front of a statue."

"Oh. Which statue?"

She hung the last dress and closed the closet. Then she walked in front of me to the window and stared out onto the street below. She stared out the window for a long time.

"The Ecstasy of Saint Teresa," she said at last. When she spoke, her back was still to me.

"What were you doing at the church?" Neither of my parents was religious.

Finally she turned and looked at me. She looked at me the same way she had looked at me back in our kitchen, just two days ago. This time I didn't arrange my face. I didn't try to look any special way.

"I was there because I was studying art history, and my project was about the bodies of female saints," she said. "You know I've always been fascinated by the stories of the saints."

"You used to tell me their stories," I said. "When I was little. At bedtime. You told me terrible stories about women getting cut up and being killed and going to heaven to be with Jesus."

"That's insane," Mom said. "I never did that."

"Yes," I said, "you did. All the time. I remember their names—Philomena and Dymphna and Agatha—"

"Don't be silly," she said. "I did no such thing. Anyway," she went on, "I was there doing research, and your father was there on vacation with his family."

"You mean with Nona and Dada?"

"No," she said. "With his first wife."

"Oh," I said, and I felt things whirring around in my head, the picture I had always imagined shifting and rearranging to make room for this new piece of information. I knew that Dad had, of course, been married to Judy before my mother. What I did not know was that Dad had still been married to her when he met my mom.

"I'm not proud of it," Mom said, but she lifted her chin in a way that made her look proud. "It was just one of those things. There he was, with his wife, taking pictures of saints they knew nothing about, and there I was, barely twenty years old, half a world away from my real life, all on my own."

"Oh," I said, again.

"I'll take you tomorrow to see the saints," Mom said, turning back to the window. Like the saints were the interesting part of her story.

I woke up in a pitch-dark room with no idea where I was, no idea who was in bed next to me breathing steadily, and no idea why my thighs felt sticky.

I woke with a gasp and the certainty that I was dead, only to recognize almost at once that I was still living. But my heart pounded hard in my chest, as if I had been chased, as if I had fallen from the sky. I reached under the covers and touched between my legs. My sleep shorts were wet.

It was my mom in bed with me, still asleep. We were in a hotel room in Rome. The bedside clock's glowing red numbers told my squinting eyes that it was 2:43, and the velvet darkness all around told me it was the middle of the night, not the afternoon.

I'd never experienced jet lag before. I didn't know that this was how it was, that you could be dead asleep one moment and more awake than you'd ever been the next, but that part of you would be missing, that part of the brain that made sense of things.

I threw back the covers and stumbled across the room. In the bathroom I felt around for the light switch and found it at last. The light flickered on and I squeezed my eyes shut against its sudden painful brightness. When I opened them again moments later, I saw the wall where I'd fumbled for the switch, I saw the white switch itself. They were smeared with blood.

Someone was dead. It was my mother. Someone had murdered her in bed next to me. I was sure of it for less than half of one second, not even long enough to scream, before I remembered that I had heard her breathing. I looked into the mirror above the sink. There I was, my hair a mess from sleep, my eyes squinted and swollen from the time change and my broken sleep. There was my body, the word—SPARKLE—on my tank top written in reverse on mirror-me. And there were my thighs, smeared like the light switch with blood.

I'd gotten my period. That was all.

I grabbed my glasses from the counter where I'd left them and then I pulled off my shorts and my underwear and peed in the toilet, watching the clear yellow stream of urine jet out from me, watching it mix with the bright-red drops of blood that splashed into the toilet bowl.

It was the first time I'd ever had my period.

At fourteen, I was the last in my small group of friends to get it. The year before I'd been anxious about it, checking in my underwear several times a day, each time hopeful, but after months of disappointment I'd given up and had decided that maybe it would be just fine if it never happened at all. And now, here it was.

There was a bidet next to the toilet. I'd never used one, but I knew what it was, and it wasn't complicated. After I flushed the toilet I scooted over to the bidet and turned the handles until lukewarm water jetted up, rinsing away the traces of blood. At the sink I rinsed out my underwear and sleep shorts, squeezing the fabric until the water turned from red to pink to clear. I hung the wet things in the shower and wondered what to do next.

Should I wake my mother? It seemed like the kind of thing a daughter would do. But first I needed to find something, like a pad. Mom's toiletries bag sat on the counter; I unzipped it and found a little pouch that held her tampons. I sat back on the toilet, fully awake now, to figure out what the hell to do with it. It took three tries to get one inside; the first one I didn't have

81

lined up right, and when I pushed on the applicator the tampon rocketed straight between my legs and into the toilet bowl.

The second one went in kind of sideways and not far enough. I pulled on the string to get it out and wrapped it in toilet paper before throwing it in the trash. The third one went in right, it seemed, but it sort of hurt. I told myself that was probably normal, since I'd never put anything inside my vagina before. And I wondered if I would be able to tell if I had torn my hymen with a tampon, since I was bleeding anyway. And then I wondered if that meant that I wasn't a virgin anymore, and if when I had sex someday if the guy would think I was a slut if I didn't bleed the first time.

I wish I could have used a pad, but Mom didn't have any in her toiletries bag and anyway it was too late now. There was a tampon in my vagina and I'd finally gotten my period and it was the middle of the night in Rome.

I went back into the bedroom. I fumbled through my suitcase for another pair of pajamas. Mom was still asleep. I almost woke her up to tell her, but at the last minute I didn't. Instead I slipped as quietly as I could back into bed, placed my glasses on the nightstand, and rolled onto my side facing away from her, pulling the covers up to my chin. Was this it, then? Was I a woman now?

Once there was a girl.

No, wait. Once there was a woman.

No. Once there was a female human, older than a girl but younger than a woman.

One day, the female human noticed something on the inside of her left arm. Halfway up, between her armpit and her elbow. It looked like a wound, but it did not hurt. She poked at it and found that her finger could slip painlessly inside.

Concerned, she showed the thing to her mother.

Her mother nodded. "I'll take you to the doctor," she said.

And so, they went. The doctor pursed his lips and shook his head. Then he took a needle and thread and sewed it closed and sent them home.

But the next day, it was as if he had never touched it. The stitches had disappeared, and it was just as it had been the day before. Also there was another, exactly like the first, on the back of her right knee. Since going to the doctor had done no good, the girl pulled on long pants and a long-sleeved shirt and went about her day, resolving to ignore the whole problem.

But the next day, and in the days that followed, more and more of the wounds-not-wounds appeared all over her body: on her stomach, in her armpits, across her back. And when the girl began her monthly cycle, blood oozed from all of them, and then she knew what they were.

Still, she hid them as best she could until a day when one appeared on her cheek, and the girl could hide them no longer. People looked at her strangely and talked about her out the sides of their mouths. Older people—men and women both—shook their heads disapprovingly. Male humans, too old to be boys but too young to be men, touched and poked at them, hard sometimes, without asking first if she minded.

The openings became the landscape of her, the definition of her, and they began to overlap and spread, crisscrossing her flesh in every direction, and the girl knew that the day was coming when they would overtake her, swallow her, and she herself would disappear.

We walked from our hotel to the Cornaro Chapel. The streets early in the day weren't crazy crowded like they'd been when we'd arrived at the hotel the day before; maybe there weren't a lot of morning people in Italy. Up and down the streets, vendors opened their doors and rolled up the metal grates that had been locked down during the night.

We were so far from Irvine, but the air felt exactly the same. Not humid, but you could tell the day was going to get warm by lunchtime.

Mom didn't need to look at a map or ask her phone for directions; she knew exactly where she was going, navigating the streets like a native Italian. She nodded her head at people as she walked, answering the occasional *"Buongiorno"* with a *"Buongiorno"* of her own, her voice easy and sure.

The Santa Maria della Vittoria looked like what it was—a big old church. Slate-gray rock, worn-down steps, big green wooden doors. Impressive, but by the time we reached it I was completely overwhelmed by all the *architecture*—all the old stuff, everywhere, that no one else even seemed to notice. There was a woman—a beggar—with a black scarf over her head, leaning on the wall of the church just to the right of the door. In front of her was a New York Giants baseball cap, several Euros and some coins inside it.

Before we went inside, Mom gave me a scarf that she pulled from her bag and told me to wrap it around myself like a skirt, over my shorts. I was preoccupied with trying to tie it at my waist as we walked through the doors, but once we were inside, I was frozen by the place in which I found myself.

Just inside the doors, I was surrounded by a degree of opulence that I had never, ever seen. Nothing in my life had prepared me for this. Every inch of the interior walls was beautiful: mottled marble pillars; gilded golden archways; ornately carved figures; a gruesomely beautiful fresco on the ceiling, filled with angels seated on clouds juxtaposed with tortured, naked people being attacked by bizarre snake creatures and surrounded by an immense gilded frame. Everywhere I looked there was beauty; spooky, awful, glorious beauty.

It was the opposite of home, a place that was clean and sanitized and standard in every way. Irvine was predictable. You didn't even have to notice the town around you, because it was completely utilitarian. Things were built to serve a purpose— form followed function, always. But what was the function of all this conspicuous wealth, all this artistic beauty? If its purpose was to incite awe, then it was a success, at least as far as I was concerned.

I walked slowly, aimlessly, unable to absorb even a fraction of what I encountered. How had the sculptors make cold, hard stone fall in gentle waves like fabric on the skirt of that angel? How had the goldsmiths shaped such fine filigree? How had the painters rendered such realistic clouds up high by the ceiling? And who on earth had had enough money to pay for all of this?

"Teresa is down there," Mom said quietly. I followed her down the left-hand side of the church. The middle of the church was filled with two parallel rows of wooden pews. A few people sat in them, looking as awestruck as I felt. A couple of older women were on their knees, hands clasped, eyes closed.

Mom stopped. "There. That's her. Saint Teresa."

It was a woman made of marble and a smiling angel above her, feathery wings spread behind him, a golden arrow held in his right hand, pulled back as if he was preparing to pierce her with it. But he was smiling, and his left hand was holding the fabric of Teresa's gown gently, lovingly, like he was about to take it off.

Her face. Head thrown back, eyes closed, mouth open. Her shoulder, curled forward as if in spasm. The tension in her fingers and bare toes. The energy, the movement captured in the stone. She was on the edge of something, in the middle of something, and I didn't know what I was seeing, I didn't know how to *feel* about what I was seeing. All I knew was that I wanted to feel like that. I wanted to be Saint Teresa, in that moment.

"Pretty wild, don't you think?" Mom stood next to me, her arms at her sides. For some reason I found myself hoping that she wouldn't reach over and touch me right then.

"You studied this in college?"

She nodded.

"What does it mean?"

"It was created by Bernini," she said. "It was a commission by Cardinal Federico Cornaro. This is his burial chapel." She pointed to the floor, near our feet. There, set into the mottled red marble floor, were two round portraits—two skeletons, one clasping its hands and seeming to smile, the other with hands raised high and its skull face twisted as if in pain.

"He's buried here?"

"Along with the rest of his family. Commissioning Bernini for this sculpture was an unusual choice." She looked at me, appraising. "Are you really interested in all this?"

I couldn't think of anything that had ever been more interesting to me than this figure, this swooning woman, this smirking angel hovering above her, arrow in hand. I had seen sculptures, of course, on field trips to museums in LA, but nothing like this. I nodded.

"Well," Mom began, "Bernini was a sculptor, of course, but he was interested in architecture and theater, as well. This is more than a statue. It's an entire installation. Look." She pointed up to the ceiling just above Teresa. Clouds seemed to float there, with light penetrating through them. I followed her hand as it gestured to a fan of golden rays behind the sculpture, glistening with sunlight. "Bernini understood the power of the stage," she said. "There's a window hidden back there, up high, to let in light and make the gold shine like that. And there—" She gestured above us to the sides of the statue. There were more sculpted figures there, which I hadn't noticed before, as all my attention was focused on Teresa and the angel. "That's the benefactor Cornaro himself, along with his family." All eight of the seated figures, four on each side, were men. Some of them were whispering to each other, some gazed intently at Teresa and the angel below, even leaning forward to get a better look. "They're seated in theater boxes, see? They're watching."

It felt creepy, these eight old men witnessing such an intimate moment between Teresa and the angel. Like they were spying on her in a moment that was meant to be private.

"And we're watching, too," Mom said. "Bernini makes us part of the audience, by positioning us here, in between these other spectators. We are witnesses right along with them."

"But . . . what's happening to her?"

Mom looked at me frankly, eyebrows raised. "She's having an orgasm."

An orgasm. I had heard the word, of course. It had to do with sex, I knew that, but Teresa wasn't having sex. She was fully clothed. The angel wasn't even touching her, just her gown.

"She didn't think of it as an orgasm, of course," Mom went on. "She thought she was being visited by God. Which, in a manner of speaking, may have been true. Read that," she said, gesturing to a plaque in front of the statue.

Beside me, on the left, appeared an angel in bodily form. . . . He was not tall but short, and very beautiful; and his face was so aflame that he appeared to be one of the highest rank of angels, who seem to be all on fire. . . . In his hands I saw a great golden spear, and at the iron tip there appeared to be a point of fire. This he plunged into my heart several times so that it penetrated to my entrails. When he pulled it out I felt that he took them with it, and left me utterly consumed by the great love of God. The pain was so severe that it made me utter several moans. The sweetness caused by this intense pain is so extreme that one cannot possibly wish it to cease, nor is one's soul content with anything but God. This is not a physical but a spiritual pain, though the body has some share in it—even a considerable share.

Pain so severe that it made her moan. Sweetness caused by the pain so extreme that she never wanted it to cease. Was that an orgasm?

"When people don't have words to describe what they're experiencing," Mom said, "they think it's magic. Or mystical. Or God."

My mother had never talked to me like this before—like a grown-up, like an equal. The subject matter was awkward and uncomfortable, but I didn't want her to stop, so I asked a question. "Like the Greeks? The way they thought thunder was caused by Zeus?"

"Exactly. People will create an explanation for a phenomenon they don't understand."

"But . . . how could Teresa have . . . you know . . . without anyone touching her?"

"The female body is a powerful and wonderful thing," she said. "Some women experience sexual climax just from thinking about it, sometimes even in dreams."

"You think Saint Teresa had a dream? Just a . . . really vivid dream where she had an . . . orgasm?"

"Either that," my mother said, "or she was actually visited by a cherubic angel with a steel-tipped sword who pierced her several times, causing overwhelming pleasure and pain all mixed together." She shrugged. "My money's on the orgasm. Eros and Thanatos, Nina," she said. "Sex and death. That's what everything reduces to, in the end."

I'd never heard my mother talk like this—about sex, or art, for that matter. She was just . . . Mom, the woman who bought my school supplies and made sure my laundry was done and liked to play tennis even in the hottest days of summer. The woman who drank vodka with diet tonic, no ice, always in her favorite crystal tumbler.

I didn't want to look at her now, with these new words between us, so I let my gaze wander over the statue. The fabric-like folds of Teresa's clothing. The light shining down from the hidden window. The angel and his spear of flame.

"So this is where you met Dad?" I felt shy asking, and I still didn't look at Mom.

"It's almost poetic, isn't it?" She was answering my question, but she wasn't talking to me anymore. Her gaze was fixed on the angel that hovered over Teresa, and I had the sense that she was seeing something there that I couldn't see. "I was photographing her for my thesis, and your dad wandered over to ask me about her."

I imagined them here, my mom as a college student and my dad as a young man, wandering away from his wife and to my mother's side.

"I told him what I knew about Teresa, and he gave me his card. He said he'd be interested in reading my project, when it was finished."

"Oh," I said. "What about . . . Judy?"

"She wasn't paying attention to him," she said. "Some women get too wrapped up in their own heads and forget they're with a man. And then the man wanders away."

We stood there side by side, watching Saint Teresa. Her toes, I saw, were flexed and strained. After a minute, Mom spoke. Her voice was brusque, like she was angry. She said, "People don't change, Nina. Remember that."

《《《

Visiting all the Roman places over the next few days—the museums and the churches, the Vatican and the Colosseum, the Spanish Steps and Trevi Fountain, the Pantheon and the Campo dei Fiori—all I could think was Eros and Thanatos, sex and death, over and over again, like a drumbeat, a terrible reckoning.

I bled for three days and then I stopped, and I did not tell my mother. I lay in a bath full of tepid water, imagining myself as Teresa, massaging myself with a rough washcloth, pretending it was the hand of God, until I came, suddenly and hard, for the first time. My mother was in the next room, and she heard me in there, she heard the sound I made, a sharp inward breath, a little high-pitched cry.

"Nina?" she asked. "Are you okay?"

It was several seconds before I could answer. "Yes," I said. "I'm fine."

I pretended not to listen to my mother on the phone with my father, pretended not to notice her red swollen eyes, pretended not to care on the nights when she said her head hurt too much to go out.

I spent those evenings on my phone, learning everything I could about Eros and Thanatos, starting with Saint Teresa and following her down a dark and twisted path that my mother had started me on.

The stories of the martyrs—the awful ways women died— I read these over and over, hearing them in my mother's voice, seeing in my brain so clearly the men who did the torturing and the killing, the men who told their stories, and the men who turned them into art, carving their flesh into marble, painting the rivers of their blood.

I saw images of their bones, preserved in wax and set on altars, transformed from women into relics.

I recited their names in my head, the virgin martyrs, at night with the lights out and the curtains drawn, our hotel room as dark and silent as Santa Maria della Vittoria must have been, just a few blocks away.

Agatha of Sicily, Christian saint and virgin martyress. Agnes of Rome, virgin martyr saint. Catherine of Alexandria, Christian saint and virgin. Valerie of Limoges, virgin martyr saint. Victoria, virgin martyr saint. Lucia, martyr saint virgin. Petronilla, virgin saint martyr. Philomena, saint virgin martyr.

Ursula, martyrvirginsaint. Cecilia, martvirgsaintyr. Dymphna, saintlyvirginalmartyr. Irene of Tomar, martyrlysaintlyvirgin. All virgins, all martyrs, all saints.

All tortured. All ruined. All dead.

《《《

We ate our meals in cafes and restaurants most of the time, and I got used to eating the way my mother did. That is to say, not often, and not much when the sun was in the sky. She would have a roll of bread and a piece of fruit for breakfast with espresso, one packet of fake sugar. There were pink packets and there were blue packets, but their contents tasted equally like poison to me.

"Coffee makes you regular," my mother told me, which was just gross. I didn't want to think about that. And it was something she never would have said if my father were with us. It was like there were different parameters for conversation, now that my father wasn't around. Sex and going to the bathroom—she never talked about anything messy or gross at home.

We spent mornings visiting landmarks and museums. I'd rent the headphones wherever they were available, listening earnestly to the self-guided walking tour, following along in guidebooks and reading all the signs, taking pictures with my cellphone that could never capture the enormity of what I was seeing.

Mom would stand, her expression inscrutable, staring at things in which I saw no meaning—the bottom step of a staircase in a museum, where the granite had been worn down by centuries of feet stepping in the same place; a crippled pigeon, one of its legs ending abruptly in a gray-tinged stump, hopping after scraps of bread thrown by greasy-fisted toddlers; the face of a broken clock in the lobby of our hotel which read, eternally, 11:59.

It was my job to provide the conversation, the levity, the propelling engine of excitement forward through Rome. I knew that it was, and I did my best, though she didn't make it easy. I pretended I didn't notice the way she'd disappear behind her eyes, and I fought to keep my tone bright and energetic, as if I could snap her back into the present moment if I managed to be perky enough.

For lunch Mom would eat a salad, usually with black olives, oil, and vinegar; I'd have salad, too, though I'd dress mine with Ranch whenever the restaurant had it.

Late afternoons brought with them glasses of wine, standing in for the vodka tonic she drank each day at home. By dinner she would be properly hungry and would finally order something of substance—pasta shells filled with cheese, spaghetti with aromatic meat sauce and a thick snowfall of Parmesan, a slab of stratified lasagna heavy with sausage. And always more wine—dark red, poured into thin-stemmed glasses, and refilled by the server from a waiting bottle before she reached the bottom.

One night, toward the end of our time in Rome, we were eating dinner at the restaurant in the lobby of our hotel. When the waiter poured her glass of wine, she motioned for him to pour one for me, as well. He obliged, tipping the bottle so a thin stream spilled into the empty cup beside my plate. When he stopped with the glass only a quarter filled, my mother motioned for him to pour more.

"You're going to get drunk eventually," Mom said. "The first time might as well be with me."

I had never given a thought to the idea of drinking alcohol, but here was a drink served to me, and here was my mother waiting for me to drink it, and I had no moral objection to the thought of getting drunk. If anything, it just seemed kind of silly that drunkenness could really happen to anyone. I had a vague belief that it was just an act people put on, silly people who wanted attention. After all, my mother drank every night, and I'd never noticed her to act any different before, during, or after.

The wine tasted terrible at first, and slightly less terrible the more I drank of it. By the time our dinner arrived—pasta, again, this time with garlicky shrimp and thick chunks of cooked tomatoes in a creamy broth—I had decided that I liked red wine quite a bit, and that drinking it made me feel older. I wondered if I looked older, holding the glass by its delicate stem, taking dainty sips between bites.

A couple at the next table, the man much older than the woman, their fingers entwined on the table between them, glanced over and smiled at me, and I smiled back, feeling a connection to them, to my mom, to the waiter who had poured my wine, to everyone.

"You look happy," my mother said. She held her own glass in her hand, and the red of the wine reflected up on her face. She looked, I thought, very European.

"I am happy," I answered, and I drank the last of my wine. Now the world was vibrating, and suddenly I heard music that I hadn't noticed before, and I couldn't tell if they'd just turned it on or if it had been playing all along.

"Are you drunk yet?"

I shook my head no. I wasn't drunk; drunk wasn't really a thing. I was just, I don't know, loose, sort of. Relaxed. Everything felt . . . better. The fork in my hand felt more solid. My mother, across from me, the red in her cheeks, looked hopeful, somehow. Everything would be okay, I felt. The warmth in my chest was proof of that. Life, it was beautiful.

Mom took another sip of her wine and then handed the glass across to me. The couple that was watching us stopped smiling.

I drank that wine, too, quickly, before the waiter came back and saw. I burped, and some of the wine and food came back up into my mouth. I swallowed it, suddenly sick, suddenly very sure that drunk was a real thing after all, and this is what it felt like.

"You don't look so happy now," Mom said.

She paid our bill and we stood up from the table. My armpits felt hot and sweaty, and I had to hold onto the edge of the table to keep from losing my balance. I closed my eyes, hoping that would make the room stop spinning, but it made it much worse, so much worse, and I opened them quickly to find my mother staring at me appraisingly.

I wanted to take her arm as we left the table, but she moved too quickly for me to grasp it, and my hand clawed at the air in the space where she had just been. When I took a step one foot crossed over the other, and I had to put all my attention into just making my way across the floor.

His voice heavy with some sort of accent and full of derision, the man at the next table said to my mother, "What kind of a parent lets her child get that drunk?"

My mother looked at the man, and then at the girl beside him. "You take care of your daughter, and I'll take care of mine," she said.

I followed her out of the restaurant and across the palatial lobby, making it all the way to the elevator before I puked into an elegant footed ashtray.

Back in our room, my mother handed me a glass of water and tucked me into bed. All night I dreamed of hurling through space, head over heels, lost and spinning, and surrounded by martyrs.

In the morning, I asked my mom through the pounding pressure of my headache, "Why did you make me get so drunk?"

"I don't know what you're talking about," she answered. "Now, get dressed. We're taking a train to Florence."

《《《

They piled up as we visited church after church, crypt after crypt, a tour of religion and violence and death. We saw other things, beautiful things, life-affirming things, but the beautiful things were slippery, sliding through me and away. The ugly stuff had hooks and claws and teeth, and it became part of me. The bodies of the virgin martyr saints arranged themselves in a line behind me, silently following me as we wound through Italy, as I read about their short lives and ugly deaths, Agnes behind Agatha, Valerie behind Catherine, on and on, eyes downcast, gentle smiles on their lips, hands clasped like schoolgirls, all just about my age. They didn't speak to me, they did not reach out to touch me, and when I slept in the hotel they formed a horseshoe around my bed and waited for me to wake, dancing through my restless dreams, bleeding from wounds to their hearts, their necks, carrying their beheaded heads, their sliced-off breasts, their gouged-out eyes.

They followed me through Italy. They watched me bathe and sleep.

And when we went to the airport, when we boarded the plane toward home, they made a line along the runway and watched me fly away from them.

At home, after we took a cab home from the airport, the empty place in the garage told me that Dad wasn't there to welcome us back. But it wasn't him I missed—it was *them*, the virgin martyr saints. Dad's parking space would remain empty for two more weeks. And then, when his car reappeared, and him with it, there would be no mention of the absence, no celebration of the return.

The day after we returned home from Italy, still groggy from the time change, I helped my mother fold the sheets fresh from the dryer.

"There is no such thing as unconditional love," my mother told me. "I could stop loving you at any time."

I thought about the virgin martyr saints. I thought about the men who had loved them, who killed them.

I thought about my mother and my father, and about my father and his first wife Judy. Her words were a warning, a gift, a benediction.

And I nodded. I believed her.

《《《

At school on Monday, I wait on the steps out front for Seth's Acura to pull into the parking lot. I wait and I wait, until the final bell has rung and I am late to class. Finally I go inside, go to class, accept the raised eyebrow I get from the chemistry teacher.

I sit in the chair I always sit in, but know that I am not the same girl who sat here on Friday.

In the cafeteria, Louise sidles up to me in the food line, her tray clacking against mine. "Are you okay?" she whispers, too loudly. "I heard what happened with you and Seth."

How could she have heard what happened? *I* don't even know what happened.

I say nothing. I take an apple and set it on my tray.

"I heard you guys broke up this weekend," she says, trying again.

I walk away, leaving my tray on the metal rails, appetite gone.

After lunch, Mr. Whitbey wants to know how our projects are coming. Each of us has had to pick a literary genre and create our own short portfolio of work in that style. Our proposals are due today, and I have a short paragraph typed up saying that I'm focusing on magical realism, but not much more than that.

So far I have written one story about a girl who grows vaginas all over her body, a couple of weird little things about chickens and eggs, and I have a growing collection of stories I've written about the deaths of virgin martyr saints, but I'm not ready to share any of it with him, or anyone.

So I hand in my too-short proposal and tell him I'm still working on figuring it out, which makes him purse his mouth and shake his head.

"Pick up the pace, Nina," he says, rapping his knuckles on my desk.

Mr. Whitbey's hands, I decide, are exactly two sizes too small for his body.

When the egg did hatch at last, it wasn't the cracking of the shell that was surprising, but rather what emerged.

All chicks are ugly at the very first. Their feathers, wet and thin, stick to their body. Their weird scaly legs are weak and useless. Their beaks look too large for their heads, and their wings are terrible stumps.

But within hours, the feathers dry and fluff and obscure their veiny thin skin and ugly skulls. The transformation is so quick that you can forgive the way they looked to start.

But this chick, from this egg, was different. Where there should have been wings, instead there were hands. Tiny fingers, each capped in a little bird claw. The hands flapped at the newly hatched chick's sides, the fingers thrumming against the wet pinfeathers of the chick's distended body.

Between the lizard-scaled legs of the tiny bird thrummed a distended orange ball—the yolk sack, improperly absorbed. It beat like a heart, like a threat, like a promise.

And the farmer, coming to check his newly hatched flock, plucked up the freakish chick at once, grasped its ugly head between his forefinger and thumb, and before the chick could peep her protest, he crushed in the thin-skulled head as easily as breaking an egg.

Life resumes, even though my heart has been cut out of my chest. On Tuesday I go to the shelter, where the familiar despair and hopelessness is sort of comforting as it exists outside of my body. Bekah lifts her chin in greeting. Her eyes stay fixed to her phone.

"Ni-na," says Stanley from his bench outside the kennels. "You're back."

"I was just here last week," I tell him, kind of sharply I guess, because his expression freezes like I've slapped him. I try again. "Hi, Stanley. It's nice to see you."

He smiles, my sharpness instantly forgotten, totally forgiven. "I missed you," he says.

"I missed you, too," I say, even though I haven't given one second of thought to Stanley or Bekah or Ruth or even the dogs since I was here last Thursday.

I grab three leashes and head for the Chihuahuas. But there's just Ginger and one of the little black males.

"Hey," I say to Stanley, "Where's the other little black guy?"

"He got adopted," Stanley says, a big, loose smile on his face. "A family took him to his forever home."

I leash up Ginger and the remaining black Chihuahua. It's

101

the uglier one, the one with a rough patch of gray hair on the top of his head and the kinked tail.

But still. One of the guys made it out. For the first time since Seth dropped me off on Saturday afternoon, I feel sort of happy.

《《《

Seth is back in school the next day. By the time I pull into the parking lot, the hood of his Acura is already cool. The print of my hand on the black metal disappears almost as soon as I lift my hand away.

Is that like a metaphor for the effect I've had on Seth? Has the mark I made on him faded, just as quickly as my handprint?

《《《

Thanksgiving comes. I don't feel thankful, and after we consume a portion of the giant dinner my mother has made, my parents and I disappear into separate rooms, just like always.

There are lots of things I am not thankful about. The very top of the list is the fact that my period doesn't come. I've finished the first pack of pills, so I should have started by now. I've never missed a period. I've never been late, even.

I know I'm pregnant before the second line appears on the test that I bought at the grocery store Thanksgiving morning, when my mom sent me out to buy more butter. I don't feel pregnant, and I don't look pregnant, but I know I am.

When the second pink line darkens parallel to the first, though, I stare at it as if it can't be true. How can it be true?

I took all of the pills.

Well. I did take them all, but it was sort of hard getting into the routine at first, and so when I missed one that first week I took two the next day, and when I forgot for a day and a half later in the month, I did my best to catch up.

I took the rest of them, though, right on time. After breakfast, on my way to school. Once I figured out that keeping them in my purse and taking one each morning while I drove made it easier to remember, I didn't miss any more.

But here is this second pink line.

At the clinic, the day after Thanksgiving, I see the same nurse practitioner. She makes me take another pregnancy test, and even though the first one at home was undeniably positive, I find myself practically praying that somehow it was defective. But no luck; though this test's second pink line slashes across the first test to form a cross rather than appearing parallel to the first, like my test from the grocery store, it's irrefutably positive.

"I'm sorry," I say, my voice choked, my eyes stinging. I'm sitting on the end of the same exam table, the stirrups splayed on either side of me, and though I'm fully dressed this time, I feel as exposed as I was the first time.

She puts her hand on my shoulder. "Honey," she says, and at her gentle touch, at the kind tone in her voice, I fall apart.

I cry until I choke, and she lets me cry, pulling me close and rocking me back and forth like I'm a baby, shhhing me, petting my hair, and I cry and cry.

I feel like the world's biggest fuck-up. I feel like such an idiot. I feel stupid and ugly and lame and so, so ashamed.

"It happens," she says, when I finally stop crying. "It happens. Now let's see how far along you are so that we can talk about your options."

She has to do an ultrasound to determine how far along my pregnancy is. In TV shows and movies, this just involves the doctor rubbing a device over the patient's stomach, but the nurse practitioner tells me that my pregnancy isn't far enough along to see this way, and that we have to do a transvaginal ultrasound. So I have to take off my jeans and underwear—though this time I do get to keep my sweater on—and lie back down on the paper-covered table. She takes out this weird penis-shaped device and rolls a condom down over it, then squirts the tip of it with some clear jelly from a bottle that looks just like a mustard container.

"Relax," she says, and I try, but I see with a jolt in my brain Seth's vibrator again, another corded device, another rubbery head.

There's a monitor, like a computer screen, next to my head.

"You don't have to look at it if you don't want to," she says. But I do look.

It's a black screen with blue lines, and as she maneuvers the probe inside my vagina, I see the inside of myself, my uterus I guess, something I've never actually given any thought to.

"There's the pregnancy," she says, and she types something with her other hand on the keyboard attached to the screen. Some numbers pop up along the side of the image.

"About five weeks' gestation," she says, and she pulls out the probe, strips it of its condom, and puts it away. She hands me some tissues to wipe between my legs. I sit up.

"That's impossible," I say. "I've only missed one period. How can I be more than a month pregnant?"

"We count the pregnancy from the first day of your last period," she says. "The embryo has only been developing for three weeks, but we count the two weeks before that, as well."

That sounds like pretty stupid math to me, but whatever. "So it's only been growing for three weeks," I say.

"Yes."

Then they put me in a room with a counselor to discuss my options.

I have options. I can continue the pregnancy. I can get an abortion.

"I don't want a baby," I say. I'm done crying now, and I absolutely know the answer to this question. I know it more surely than any question I've ever answered, ever.

"Okay," says the counselor. "This is California, so you aren't required to have parental permission to move forward, but we do recommend that you consider having someone with you. It's not a good idea to process all these feelings on your own. Is there someone safe you could talk to?"

I think about Louise, and how she already knew that Seth had dumped me, even though he never actually said the words. I think about my mother, and all the times she put away her crystal tumbler, all the babies she wanted but couldn't have.

"I have someone," I say, though the person who springs to mind surprises me.

The counselor, Angie, tells me about my abortion choices, which is news to me, that there are choices. I've seen the old movies, and I'm already prepared to put my feet back in those awful stirrups, I'm ready to let the nurse practitioner crank me open and scrape inside.

"This early in the pregnancy," Angie says, "you can choose to have either an in-clinic or a medical abortion."

I've been staring at the orange fish she has tattooed on her forearm, counting its scales, but at this I look up. "What's the difference?"

"An in-clinic abortion requires inserting a speculum into your vagina, injecting numbing medication, and then dilating your cervix. Then the practitioner will insert a tube through your cervix into your uterus. A suction device will be used to empty your uterus. The entire procedure should take about five or ten minutes."

"What's the other choice?"

"A medical abortion. This involves taking two medications—one here in the clinic, called Mifepristone, another at home, called Misoprostol, twenty-four hours later. The abortion will begin after you take the first pill. Mifepristone blocks the hormone progesterone, which your body makes to support the pregnancy. Misoprostol causes the uterus to empty."

"I want to do that one," I say.

"The medical abortion?"

I nod.

"Okay," she says, and she pulls a pamphlet out of her desk, handing it to me. It's all about abortions, of course. "It's normal if you feel hot after taking the first pill. And we strongly recommend that you have someone to support you for a few hours after you take the second medication. You may have some cramping, and it can be intense. For some women, it's quite painful. Women who have experienced miscarriages liken this experience to that. You might also have nausea and diarrhea."

"How much will I bleed?"

"That's different from woman to woman," Angie says. "Some women experience heavy bleeding and expel large clots and tissue, and other women report their bleeding to be about the same as the heaviest day of their period." My periods have always been light and short, with no really painful cramps or anything. I wonder if that means that my abortion will be easy, too. My abortion. Two words I never thought together before.

I flip through the pamphlet. There are images of women consulting with other women in white medical jackets. There's a white woman, and a black woman, and a Latina. Equal-opportunity abortion.

"Most women abort within four to five hours after taking the second medication," Angie says. "For some women, it takes longer, up to a few days. And it's important that you don't use tampons until your next period, and avoid intercourse for at least a week."

I laugh, a quick unhappy bark. "No problem there," I say. Then I look up.

Angie's face is kind. She's not smiling or frowning, but her brown hands are resting on the desk side by side, flat and calm. Her short dark hair arches back from her face in a wave. Her eyes are dark, too, and they look straight at me. "Do you have any questions?" she asks.

"No," I say. Then, almost immediately, "Have you ever had an abortion?"

Jesus. That's not the kind of question you ask someone.

But Angie doesn't look offended. "Yes," she says. "I'm not really supposed to talk about my own experiences, but yes. Twice. Once the kind you're having, with the Abortion Pill, and once before that, the surgical kind."

I don't ask why, but Angie smiles like she knows I'm wondering.

"The first time, I was a little younger than you. My boy-friend and I were sexually active, but the condom we were using broke. I should have come to a place like this and gotten the Morning After Pill, but I didn't even know it existed. By the time I admitted to myself that my period was never going to come, I was thirteen weeks pregnant. Too far along for the Abortion Pill. The second time was just last year."

"Oh," I say. Then, "Were you sorry? Are you sorry?"

Angie shakes her head. "I don't believe in God," she says, "But if I did, I'd thank him every day for both of my abortions."

I sign some papers, and I swipe my bank card to pay for it, thinking that this certainly wasn't what I had intended to do with my birthday money, but oh well. I wonder what happens to girls who don't have $659 they can get their hands on this easily.

Then Angie walks me back into the exam room, and she hugs me. Her skin smells like vanilla.

The nurse practitioner comes back in. She pops open a pill packet and taps a single white pill, as innocuous-looking as an aspirin, into a little clear plastic cup. She fills a second cup with water.

"You'll need to come back for a follow-up ultrasound next week," she says before she hands me the pill. "It's very important. We'll need to make sure that your uterus has expelled everything. Otherwise there's a risk of infection. Okay?" Her face is very serious. This is important.

"Okay."

She nods. "The rest of the prescription is here," she says, unclipping a little white pharmacy bag from her clipboard and handing it to me. "In twenty-four hours, you'll take this medication. You don't swallow it, though. There are four small Misoprostol tablets. You'll put them in your mouth between your lower lip and your gum and hold them there until they dissolve—about thirty minutes. Okay?"

"Okay," I say again.

"There's another medication in there, too, to help with the nausea you will probably feel tomorrow, and I recommend you take Midol to help with the cramping."

I nod. "Anything else?"

"That's everything. The abortion begins after you take this first pill. A pregnancy can't survive without the progesterone to support it. So take a few minutes if you'd like, for yourself, before you take it. Then make a follow-up appointment at the front desk before you leave."

I don't need a few minutes. I pick up the cup that holds the pill and tip it into my mouth and swallow it down with the water.

I wipe my mouth with a tissue from the box on the counter. "Thank you," I say.

«««

I stop at the drugstore on my way home to buy maxi pads and Midol. While I'm at it I pick up some chocolate chip cookies and a few bags of microwave popcorn. Before I drive home, I text Bekah.

Hey R U BZ 2morrow

She texts back almost immediately. *No whats up*

It feels weird to text about the abortion. So I call her.

"Hey," she says.

"Hey."

The words are almost painfully hard to get out—"I'm pregnant and I'm taking these pills so that I can stop being pregnant and the doctor said I shouldn't be alone"—but I say them and then feel this jolt of fear that she'll hate me or judge me or ask me how I was dumb enough to get pregnant in the first place.

But she says none of these things. Instead she answers, "It'll be like a slumber party!" Her voice is ironically chirpy.

"I did buy snacks," I say.

"I'll bring nail polish," she says, facetiously or sincerely, I have no idea.

Either way is fine with me. I'm just glad she's going to come.

《《《

It turns out that it's a perfect weekend to have an abortion because my parents decide to drive up the coast for a couple of nights, something they do every now and then. They used to hire the lady who cleans for us to sleep over, but now that I can drive, they just tell me to be good and keep my phone charged, and to answer if they call. They put a few twenties on the kitchen counter, which I won't need to spend because my mother has stocked the fridge and there are still leftovers from Thanksgiving dinner, anyway.

They leave.

I text Bekah and she says she's on her way.

Part of my brain wants to think about Seth and how we still haven't talked and all the ways I feel about that, but I push the whole mess to the corner of my mind. One thing at a time.

There's this writer who writes about writing. She says that when her brother was a kid, he had to do this bird project for school. He was supposed to draw a whole bunch of birds and write description of them. It was intended to be a semester-long project, but instead he waited until the last minute, and the night before the project was due, he started freaking out about how he couldn't possibly get it done in time. Then their dad, all calm and kind, told her brother to just take it bird by bird. One thing at a time.

"Bird by bird," I say, and I pop the four pills out of their four individual plastic bubbles, and I slip them into the space between my lip and my gums, imagining them as four little eggs.

At first when she began to feel sick she thought it was something she ate. It didn't occur to her that perhaps the problem was instead something she had done, not until she was so sick that she could no longer hold it back, hold it down, hold it in.

Not vomit. She heaved and choked and then up it came. It was slick with saliva, but solid at its core. And as soon as it rose up from her throat and into her mouth and then out onto the light yellow duvet of her bed, she felt much better, indeed.

It was pellet shaped, about as big as a chicken egg, a mass of feathers and hair. At first she poked at it with a pen, wondering that she could have produced such a thing—was it possible that this had grown inside her?—but then she set the pen aside and picked at the thing with her nails, her fingers, her hands.

The hair was her own, that was clear—dark brown, almost black, and long, tangled together in an impossible snarl. Woven in were feathers—white feathers, brown feathers, pinfeathers and tail feathers. These she pulled free from the knotted hair and laid in a row, side by side on the yellow duvet.

And then there were the bones—little bones, like the bones inside a Barbie doll, if a Barbie doll was made of human stuff—strangest of all a tiny skull, with sockets for eyes, a hole where a nose could be.

And teeth—incisors, molars, canines. Some bright white, others stained yellowish as if from time and use.

She pulled free the teeth, and laid them beneath the bones that she had placed beneath the feathers that she had pulled from the pellet that she had disgorged from somewhere deep inside.

The sight of it—of all of it—fascinated and disgusted her, both at exactly the same time, and to the same degree.

And when she had finished examining all the separate parts, she pushed the teeth and the bones and the feathers back into the tangled web of hair and she slipped the whole of it beneath her pillow and rested her head and pulled the duvet up to her chin and she closed her eyes and slept.

Almost as soon as I put the pills in my mouth I start feeling sick to my stomach, even though I've already taken the anti-nausea medication. I can't tell if I feel sick because I really feel sick or just because of everything. They're bitter, the pills, terribly so, but I force myself to let them disintegrate. They turn to chalky mush against my gums.

Bekah gets there before the pills have melted all the way, and I sort of mumble, "I can't talk yet but come in." She's got a new piercing on her eyebrow, actually pretty demure, and she's holding two cloth bags, which she takes straight to the kitchen.

"Nice place," she says, thunking the bags down on the counter. She looks around, running her hand along the cold marble countertop.

Bekah lives in Santa Ana not far from the shelter. I've never been to her place, and come to think of it I don't think she even has a car. She rides her bike to the shelter.

When the pills have dissolved as much as I can stand to let them, I drink a glass of water, swishing the first few sips around my mouth before I swallow, trying to clear away the taste.

Done. It's done.

"Thanks for coming," I say. "How did you get here, anyway?"

"I took the bus," Bekah said. "I had to transfer once and walk a mile or so after I got off the second bus, but it was no big deal. It just took like an hour and a half."

"I could have picked you up." Jesus, I am such a dick.

She shrugs. "I don't mind the bus," she says. "You've just got to plan your day around the schedule."

She's unloading the bags onto the counter. There are cans of chicken broth, and Lipton's noodle-soup mix, and an onion and a bunch of carrots and some celery and a box that says *Matzo Ball Mix.* "You've got eggs and vegetable oil, right?"

I nod.

"Good. I figured you would."

"Are you going to cook?"

"I'm making you my Nana's matzo-ball soup." When everything is unloaded, she goes to the sink and washes her hands. "Do you want to go lie down or something?"

I shake my head.

"Then sit down at the table," she says. "You're making me nervous, standing there staring at me."

"Can I help?"

"Nope."

So I go to the table and sit down, which actually seems like a really good idea as soon as I'm sitting. I feel sicker and I start to wonder what happens if I throw up. Will I have to go back to the clinic for more pills?

Bekah opens and shuts a bunch of cabinets and gets out a mixing bowl, the vegetable oil, a cutting board, and a chopping knife. Then she gets the eggs from the fridge and a fork from the cutlery drawer. She pulls out the turkey carcass, too, and sets it to the side.

She cracks open two of the eggs into the bowl and pours a long stream of oil in after them without measuring. The sight of the slimy, dripping yolks makes me close my eyes and take deep breaths. They bring to mind the stories I've been writing about chickens and eggs and they remind me, too, of my own insides, what is happening right now inside my body.

When I reopen my eyes, Bekah is whipping the eggs and oil together with the fork. Then she opens the matzo-ball box, pulls out a white paper bag, taps it twice against the side of the counter with a practiced air, and rips it open. She pours the matzo mix into the egg and oil mixture and stirs it all together. When she's done, she takes the bowl over to the fridge and puts it inside.

Then she pulls two pots out from the cabinet under the stove. She fills one with water, covers it, and sets it to boil and then pours some oil into the other one and sets it on low. She rinses the vegetables in the sink and shakes off the excess water, then picks up the knife and begins cutting them up, peeling and chopping the onion first, then the carrots, then the celery, adding each vegetable to the now-hot oil and stirring the whole thing together with a wooden spoon she's taken from the canister next to the stove.

The kitchen fills with the scent and sound of sautéing vegetables. I sit very still. I watch Bekah cook. When the vegetables have softened, she opens the cans of chicken broth and pours them in. The broth sizzles as it hits the bottom of the pot. Then she pulls the turkey onto her cutting board and takes the knife to it, chopping the meat into bite-sized cubes and adding them to the soup.

"When I was little, Nana would make me matzo-ball soup every time I was sick," Bekah says. "She'd come over to our house with bags just like these full of all the ingredients, and I could smell the soup all the way from my bed. It always made me feel better, even before I had a single bite."

The water is boiling. Bekah goes to the fridge and brings out the bowl of matzo-ball mix. She uncovers the pot of water and scoops up a small glob of the thickened mixture from the bowl. She cups it in her hands and rolls it around, forming a ball, before dropping it into the boiling water. She does this again and again, scraping the bowl for the last of the matzo mix. Then she puts the lid on the pot and turns the flame down to low.

"Twenty minutes," she tells me, and shakes the Lipton noodle soup mix into the other pot with the vegetables, turkey pieces, and chicken broth. "Then I'll put the matzo balls in with the rest of the soup and we'll eat."

As she's chopped apart the rest of the turkey, Bekah has pulled free the wishbone, and she carries it over to the table where I'm sitting. "Make a wish," she says, and holds it out to me.

The two limbs of the bone bow out like legs. I take hold of one. Bekah grips the other. I close my eyes. I search for a wish. I pull. The bone is soft, not ready for wishes. It should have spent a few days drying out. It bends as we pull on it, and I think maybe it won't come apart, but then, with a quiet gasp, it cracks and breaks. I open my eyes. Bekah holds a bone fragment; the rest of the wishbone is in my hand.

"You win."

I spin the bone. The edge of the broken limb is sharp. It could be the finger bone of a long-dead saint.

My stomach lurches and tightens, a wave of cramps doubling me, and suddenly I need to go to the bathroom very, very badly.

"I'll be upstairs," I tell Bekah, dropping the bone onto the table. "Eat anything you want or watch TV or something."

I don't mean to be rude but actually making it to the bathroom in time doesn't feel like a certainty, and I rush up the stairs and down the hall, unbuttoning my pants as I go.

On the toilet I feel my bowels loosen and my thighs are shaking, and I flush the toilet twice before I'm ready to wipe, and when I do wipe there's red on the toilet paper.

I start the shower and strip out of my clothes, and I stand there under the hot stream of water with my eyes closed for a long, long time.

By the time I get out, the cramping feels like a bad case of the stomach flu. I wrap myself in a towel and sit back down on the toilet. My wet hair drips a semicircle of droplets onto the tile floor around me.

There's a knock on the door. "Nina? Are you okay? Do you need something?"

"No," I call out quickly, not wanting Bekah to come in. I didn't lock the door in my rush.

She's quiet for a moment, but I can feel her there. Then, "Nina, come on. Let me help."

I feel tears sting in my eyes, and I don't know why.

"Okay," I say.

I tell her where to find the maxi pads and ask her to look in the top drawer of my dresser for the biggest pair of underwear she can find. I ask her to bring me my robe, which is hanging on the back of my bedroom door.

She comes into the bathroom minutes later, holding all the things I asked for. She's opened the bag of maxi pads and fitted one into the crotch of my underwear, and she hands it to me while I'm still sitting on the toilet.

I pull on the underwear and flush the toilet. Then when I'm standing she gives me my robe. I pull it on and tie its belt, letting the towel drop to the floor.

"Do you want to go lie down?"

I shake my head. "I'm not sick."

We go downstairs and Bekah ladles out two bowls of soup. I sit in front of mine and breathe in the steam that rises from it.

Bekah sits across from me. She slices into one of her matzo balls with the edge of her spoon and blows on it before she puts it in her mouth.

I do the same. The matzo ball doesn't look like it's going to taste very good; it's this heavy, pockmarked, uneven whitish sphere. But it's soaked up the broth like a sponge would, and it's hot and tender and flavorful, salty and filling.

I eat the whole bowl.

"Is your grandmother Jewish?" I ask.

"Mm-hm. My whole family is."

"Are you religious?"

"Sort of," Bekah says. "My grandparents on my father's side are Hungarian Jews. They're not Orthodox or anything, though. Not for a long time. My mom's family is full of right-wing Christian nut jobs. They were super pissed when she married my dad and converted. They said it could never work."

"And your parents proved them wrong?"

Bekah snorts. "Nope. They were separated by the time I was four, when my mom was eight months pregnant with my little sister. She didn't stay married, but she stayed a Jew."

"Oh," I say. "Why'd they break up?"

"You know," Bekah says. "All the reasons people break up. They fought all the time. My dad drank too much. They probably lied to each other."

Are those the reasons people break up? I think of Seth and me. We didn't fight. Neither of us drank, except occasionally at parties. I had never lied to Seth. Had he lied to me? I would have forgiven him if he had.

I feel a rush of warmth between my legs, a heavy pulse of blood. It strikes me that maybe this is a lie of omission, my not telling Seth about the abortion. But I am not sorry.

I stand up to go deal with the blood, and I feel more of it coming out.

"Um," says Bekah, and she's looking at the chair I was sitting on.

There's blood on it. "Oh, God. I'm sorry," I say, and I grab the roll of paper towels from the counter.

"It's okay," Bekah says. "I'll get it."

"No, I'll do it," I say. "I don't want you to clean up after me."

"I'm here to help, remember?" Gently, Bekah takes the roll of paper towels.

I go back upstairs. This time, I lock the bathroom door.

I strip naked, throw my robe in the sink, and run cold water over the back of it where the blood has soaked through. The underwear and maxi pad I throw together into the trash. I sit on the toilet and I cramp and bleed, liquid blood and blood clots, something that might be tissue.

I run a bath. I slide into the water and watch as long strands of blood weave through it. The blood is terrible. The blood is beautiful. I close my eyes. The temperature of the water is just the same as my skin, as my blood. I can't tell my insides from my outsides. I float.

《《《

Bekah stays with me all day. By the time it's dark outside, the bleeding has slowed to my normal period flow. Bekah makes popcorn and we climb into my bed and watch the beginning of this romantic drama set in the 1800s, but it's boring and depressing so we switch it to something funny.

Even that, though, we mostly ignore. We eat the popcorn. Mom's cat wanders in and hops up onto the bed. She purrs loudly, her begging purr.

"She likes popcorn," I say, and Bekah tosses her a kernel.

"What's her name?"

"Hannah."

"Hey, there, Hannah," Bekah says, rubbing her fingers together. The cat comes over and rubs her head against Bekah's hand. "She's a pretty cat."

Hannah is a big long-haired tabby with white whiskers and an extremely fluffy tail.

"We got her a couple of years ago," I tell Bekah. "My dad had always said no to animals—he's allergic—but the summer before I started high school he and Mom had some troubles, I guess, and she and I went away to Italy for a few weeks. Actually, it was supposed to be their anniversary trip. A couple of weeks after we got home, Dad came back, and he had Hannah with him. Like, an apology present, I guess."

"What do you think the problem was with them?"

I shrug, running my hand down Hannah's back. But an image flashes in my mind, like a snapshot, of the couple that was at the restaurant that night I got drunk in Italy. The much-older man. The younger woman. My dad with Judy, then my mother.

I turn up the volume of the movie. We settle back against the pillows. Hannah circles and curls up in Bekah's lap, her tail draped around her own neck like a scarf.

I have to go back to school on Monday. I can't use a tampon, so I've got a pad on, but the bleeding is way lighter now, and the cramps are gone.

In the morning Bekah sends me a text checking to see how I am feeling.

Better, I write. *Thank you.*

I type out *thank you* instead of *thx* because I want her to know that I really mean it, and she understands because she sends back *You are welcome*.

In the parking lot, I see Seth's car. And I see Apollonia Corado, standing in my spot in the universe, just in front of Seth, pushed up against the trunk of his car, his arms draped around her waist, her chin tilted toward him, her hair in two braids down her back like thick black snakes.

I'm not surprised. Not at all. I park my car as far away from Seth's Acura as humanly possible and go to class.

Over the weekend someone took down all the Thanksgiving stuff and painted fake snow in the corners of the windows. Construction paper pine trees are on every door. It feels like the crowded hallways part for me as I pass through them. It feels as though everyone is watching me, and I wonder with a sick jolt if I've bled through my jeans, if that's why they're whispering and staring.

But then I remember the parking lot, Seth and Apollonia, and I get what this is about. Do they want to see me cry? Do they want to see me shake with rage? What do they want from me?

What do they want?

But then, a tiny unhatched voice from deep inside my brain whispers a different question: What do *I* want?

《《《

My follow-up appointment at Planned Parenthood is on Wednesday. My parents have been back in town since Monday night, and for some reason my mother has decided that we need to spend time together as a family, which she does every now and then, and it's usually okay except this is a bad week for her to get all involved. I tell her that I have to go to the library to work on my English project, and I won't be home in time for dinner.

"Well, do you have to go *tonight*?" she asks. "The library tonight, you were at the shelter yesterday and you're going back tomorrow. It feels like we never see you anymore. Isn't your debt to society paid yet?"

She barely ever mentions the fact that my work at the shelter is the penance I accepted rather than being suspended after what happened last year. And I don't bother to tell her that, actually, I could have stopped going to the shelter last month. My time has been served. My record has been expunged. I go to the shelter because I like it there, because even with the smell of urine and depressing Play Yard and frightened animals, it's better than being at home. And more than that—I'm needed there, at the shelter. Even if the dogs are damned, I can do something there to make things just a little bit better for them. No one needs me at home.

Instead I say, "Sorry, Mom. We can do family dinner on Friday, okay?"

At the clinic, the nurse practitioner does another ultrasound. I lie back, for a third time, on the same paper-covered table. This time, my uterus looks like an empty cave.

"Great," she says. "You're no longer pregnant."

Tears fill my eyes and spill down the sides of my face, into my ears.

The nurse practitioner gives me some tissues to wipe off the jelly and some more for my face. I sit up.

"How do you feel?" she asks.

How do I feel? I reach inward, searching with blind hands for the word that matches my emotion.

"Relieved," I say.

"Good." Her smile is gentle, and kind, and I wonder why I didn't think she was pretty the first time I saw her. Then she says, "We need to talk about birth control moving forward, okay?"

"My boyfriend broke up with me," I say. It's the first time I've said it out loud. "I don't need any birth control."

"Ah," she says, and she pulls up her chair to sit close to me. "Was it because of the pregnancy?"

"I don't know why he broke up with me. Maybe because of this other girl. Maybe it's because I'm a horrible person. I don't know." I picture the Bridge to Nowhere and the people diving off of it. I hear Seth's voice asking me if I would jump. And I wonder for the first time if maybe there was no right answer to that question—if no matter what I said that day, he would have been done with me.

She smiles sympathetically. "Breakups can be hard," she says. "And you're not a terrible person." We sit together for a minute, me wiping my tears. Eventually I blow my nose. Then she says, "You still need birth control."

I don't answer.

She continues, "I know right now it feels like you're never going to want to have sex again. Between breaking up with your boyfriend and the abortion, sex is probably among the very last things you'd want right now. But that will change. And you need protection."

"I'll buy some condoms if that happens," I say.

"Condoms are great," she says. "In an ideal world you'd use a condom every time, in addition to hormonal birth control. Condoms are the best way to prevent disease. But condoms break, and sometimes people don't make the best decisions in the heat of the moment, and a condom is something the man puts on."

I have a headache. I don't want to talk about this. But she's right.

"Okay," I say. "Can I get the shot?"

"There are a couple of other options, too," she says. "There's a patch you wear, like a sticker, that you change once a week. And there's an implant, if you'd like to learn more about that, which is effective for three years. I have one myself." She shrugs her left arm out of her white coat, pushes up the sleeve of her black shirt, and shows me the inside of her upper arm. "Here," she says, and lets me feel the slim strand of the hormonal implant just under her skin. Her skin is soft and pale. I can see the bluish outlines of several veins there, too. She has a small, flat mole just above the inside of her elbow. Her skin is warm.

We sit there together, her arm turned out and bared to me, my hand on her skin.

"This is my third time with one of these," she says after a moment, rolling down her sleeve and shrugging back into her coat. "I think they're great."

She hands me a pamphlet all about the implant. "It's totally up to you," she says. "I'm here to give you information and access, but this is your decision. You can take any of these options, or you can decide to do nothing at all."

I don't have any desire to have sex with anyone right now, not even Seth. I can't imagine a time when I'll want to allow any guy to put his penis inside me. I'm still sitting on one of the awkward, uncomfortable maxi pads, I'm still bleeding from my abortion. But that abortion was the kindest, best thing I have done for myself in as long as I can remember. It was probably the best decision I have ever made—maybe the best decision I will ever make.

So I get the implant.

《《《

Apollonia is having a birthday party. She's turning seventeen on December 13, and she's going to have a dinner party at her house, catered. Her parents told her she could invite a dozen people, no more.

Louise has called to tell me this. Her voice is apologetic, but there's this vibration of excitement, too, because she has received one of the twelve invitations. She's been chosen.

"You don't mind if I go, do you, Neen? I mean, it's not like she stole Seth from you. You guys were already broken up when they got together. And anyway, she had him first."

Is she asking my permission?

"It sounds like fun," I say. "Do you know what you're going to wear?"

"The invitation said it was black tie, so something fancy." Louise is gushing now with excitement, with having made the cut, with having been selected. "I was thinking of going to Lavish to pick something out. I don't suppose you'd . . .

"Yeah, I don't think so, Louise."

"No, yeah, of course. I totally understand. I shouldn't have asked."

There's a long uncomfortable pause. We both want to hang up. Finally I put her out of her misery. "Listen, I've got to go help my mom with something. Have fun at the party." I press End.

Only twelve invitations.

《《《

The day of Apollonia's party, a Friday night, I pick up an extra shift at the shelter. Bekah wants to leave early to make it to a movie with her boyfriend, so I offer to stay until we close up for the night. Actually, it's a relief to have something to do.

It's raining. It barely ever rains here. We've been going through this epic drought for five years, but it's not like it really affects me on a day-to-day basis. I mean, the ocean still has plenty of water in it, if I ever make it out for an afternoon to the beach, and our sprinklers still click on at three in the morning every few days, keeping our little patch of lawn waxy green.

But when it *does* rain, it triggers some switch in my brain. Suddenly I'm taking these deep gulps of air, smelling the wetness, the dirt, the leaves, all the things that are usually too dry to have a smell at all but, dampened by rainwater, come to life.

Stanley is away visiting his mother's cousins in Canada. He'll be gone from now through Christmas. I sit at Bekah's post behind the counter playing Spider Solitaire on the main computer. Ruth's in the back somewhere, dealing with paperwork.

I feel okay. Not great, but not terrible. Okay.

When the door is pushed open, a cold gust of air blows in, a wet blast of winter. I shiver and zip my sweatshirt before I even look up.

There are three of them. Two guys and a girl, who hangs behind. They're all white, like, really white, pale. The guy carrying the box has about an inch of blond roots at the top of dyed-black hair.

"We found this dog," the other guy says. He's probably the oldest, maybe twenty-five, and he's the biggest. His face is sort of loose, like an undercooked egg. And he's tall—gangly tall, not rangy tall. Every part of him could have been attractive. There's nothing wrong with his nose, or his eyes, or the slant of his shoulders. In pieces, he is handsome. But in real life, the way everything comes together . . . he isn't. "We think he was hit by a car."

The other guy, the one with the blond roots, the one carrying the box, starts to say something, but the tall guy cuts him off. "We just thought the best thing to do would be to bring him here," he says. Then he takes the box from the other guy, slides it onto the counter.

It's a cardboard box, damp and limp from the rain, and the flaps across the top are crossed and tucked together to hold it shut. There's a sound, a low, constant whine from inside. My stomach roils with nausea. I don't want to open the box. I don't want to see the dog. I don't want this dog to exist.

Still, my hands go to the flaps. The cardboard feels mushy. I peel open the box.

The whine gets higher and louder as light enters the box. It's the sound of total fear. Wet black eyes look up at me from a small brown face. The dog is terrified, I can tell, but she doesn't move at all. She can't, I can tell she can't, or she would. She would try to get away. She's a young dog, not full grown, some sort of terrier mix, maybe twelve or fifteen pounds. There's some blood smeared on the side of the box, and it stinks of urine.

I look up when I hear the door opening again, and I see them leave—the guys already out, and then the girl, half through the door but stopping to look back. Her face—it looks like the dog's, for a flash, the look in her eyes—and then she says, "Sorry," and she disappears out into the rain, the door closing fast behind her.

They are supposed to fill out forms. They are supposed to sign a release. But I don't go after them. Instead I scoop up the soggy box, the limp, broken dog, and I head into the back of the shelter.

"Ruth," I yell, and she appears almost at once. My voice is panicked, and her face reflects it.

"What's the matter?" Then she sees the box in my hands.

"They say she was hit by a car, but they just took off, they left."

Ruth takes the box from me. My arms are wet from holding it, the front of my sweatshirt damp, and I smell like the dog's pee. She carries the box into an exam room and I follow, empty-handed and shaking. She sets it on the table.

The dog's high-pitched whine hasn't stopped. It goes up another level, it is awful, it is the sound of pain and fear and absolute hopelessness.

"What do you think?" she says, looking at the dog, not me.

"They were lying," I say, completely sure. "They didn't find her like this."

Ruth nods. She leaves the room, and I know where she's going—to the locked case where they keep the medication.

I don't want to see the dog. I don't want to touch the dog. But I go over to the box. I reach inside, and I place my hand as gently as I can on the top of her head, just between her ears, the one place that I'm pretty sure isn't broken.

"Good girl," I say, soft and low. "Good girl, it's okay, it'll just be a minute. Good girl."

Ruth comes back in, the syringe in her hand, and she's the fucking angel of mercy. She finds a vein right away and presses down on the plunger. I keep my hand on the dog's head.

The whimpering quiets and softens and then stops. The rapid rise and fall of breaths from the broken body cease. Her eyes don't close but the shine fades away, and then she's dead.

I'm crying. Ruth's crying too, even though nothing makes Ruth cry.

"We did the right thing," she says, to herself or to me, I don't know, but I nod. She puts an arm around my shoulder and hugs me roughly.

Later, after she calls the police to report what's happened, after I've given the best description I can of all three of them, after the vet has come and taken x-rays of the dog's body—all four paws shattered, back broken in three places, hips crushed, likely systemic torture and abuse—after they've taken pictures of her body, I head home.

The rain has stopped. I walk across the parking lot and slide behind the wheel of my car. I sit there, smelling like dog urine and my own sweaty fear. I see behind my eyes those other eyes—first the black eyes of the dog, the way they went from shiny and full of fear to flattened black and dead but no longer in pain, at least—and then the other eyes. The eyes of the girl as she ducked out the door and into the rain. Those eyes were afraid, too.

I start my car. I pull out of the parking lot. The streets are unusually clear and I make it back to Irvine in less than twenty minutes. I drive very carefully, even more carefully than usual. It starts to rain again just as I turn into my neighborhood, a soft mist. For once, I hope my parents are home. I want to tell them about what happened. I want them to listen and hold me and pet my hair.

But when I open the garage door, there are two vacant black spaces where their cars should be.

I kick off my boots in the kitchen. I walk through the vast and silent house, I climb the meaningless staircase, I go into my room and strip naked, smelling the rain and the dead dog's urine as I pull my T-shirt off over my head. I shower.

Standing wrapped in a towel, I pull open the top drawer of my dresser. I look down at the tank tops and soft flannel pants. I think about putting them on and crawling into my bed. Pulling my comforter up over my head. But it's early, though it feels too late by far, and I am not tired. I close the drawer.

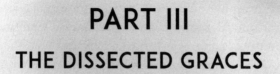

PART III
THE DISSECTED GRACES

When I was fourteen, after we'd finished touring Rome, with me still hung over from the wine my mother wouldn't talk about serving me, we had taken a train to Florence. It was, my mother said, her favorite city in Italy.

It felt more like a real place where people could actually live. It was still old, but without the giant ancient stuff like the Colosseum and Pantheon and Vatican City, there was room to breathe. In Rome, there were too many wars, too many stories, too many bodies stacked one atop another to ever disentangle.

The saints followed me to Florence, of course, the whole long line of them. But they were quiet, and they were beginning to feel as much a part of me as my shadow, and just as harmless.

Mom took me to La Specola, the oldest public museum in Europe.

"Look," she said.

The saints looked with me. The floor was made of worn bricks set on an angle in a crisscross pattern. The windows were covered with dark green curtains, the kind you might find in a restaurant, and they were pulled tight to protect the displays. Weird florescent tubes lined the ceiling, flooding the room in harsh white light. Every wall was covered with framed pictures and specimens, all anatomical. Beneath the pictures were wooden shelves painted the same shade of green as the curtains. They were full of glass boxes. Each box held a dis-embodied part—feet and organs and hands—but my focus was drawn to three long glass cases in the center of the room.

The cases themselves were beautiful, raised hip high on delicately turned wooden legs. They weren't just cases, though; they were coffins. In each of them was a tufted mattress—the ones on the ends, purple, the one in the middle, white. Upon each mattress was an artistically rumpled sheet, and upon each sheet was a woman's naked body.

"Are they real?" I whispered, as if I might wake them. But even if they had been real, they could not have been alive, not even in a Snow White trance, for their skin was flayed open, chest to pubic bones, and their guts spilled out, as artistically rumpled as the sheets.

"They're art," Mom said. "Wax sculptures."

I circled the figures. Rapunzel-long hair flowed from their heads, this one dark and loose, that one twisted into blond braids. Their cheeks and lips flushed red with life; their glass eyes, blue and green and brown, looked up at me or maybe just beyond my shoulder, to the saints who followed me. They had jewels fastened around their throats, woven in their hair. Each reclining model held her right leg slightly bent, curved alluringly. Each model grasped at her sheet. Each model's head tipped up and back.

"But what are they?" I asked again.

"They're the Dissected Graces."

I had no idea what that meant, but it made perfect sense.

"They're anatomical models, of sorts," Mom said. "They were sculpted by Clemente Susini. The idea was that medical students could study these instead of corpses. They wouldn't rot, they didn't stink, and, of course, they were beautiful. A perfect woman. These three are a set—*Le Grazie Smontate*, or The Dissected Graces. You'll notice," she went on, circling the middle coffin, "that they look almost alive. The color of their skin. Their expressions."

"Their coffins look like beds," I said, "the way their heads are on pillows."

"Yes," Mom said. "Look at the way they're posed. Everything is purposeful, Nina. There are no accidents."

I saw their open hands, their gently curved fingers. I saw their soft thighs, the hair curled between them.

"If they were just for learning about the body, they wouldn't need long hair and jewelry," I said.

"Right," Mom answered. She sounded pleased, like I was a dog who had performed its trick just right. "But here we have the intersection of love and death again. Of beauty"— she gestured to the figure's sweet face—"and gore." Her hand pointed down to the flayed-open chest, the erupting intestines.

"Eros and Thanatos," I murmured.

"Exactly." Mom tapped the top of the glass coffin.

One figure, the one with long blonde hair, some of it braided, some of it loose, looked like the sculpture of Saint Teresa. Her legs seemed to writhe, either in pleasure or pain, and her hands clutched the sheet beneath her. Her head was tossed back, shoulders thrust forward, and the shiny worms of her waxy guts framed the deepest center of her.

"She doesn't look dead," I said, "but she doesn't look alive, either."

"Look at this one's nipple," Mom said, and I turned my attention to where she pointed. This figure's chest was splayed open, the breasts flipped almost upside down, like open doors. I felt Saint Agatha twitch behind me with recognition of her twin. "See the color of it? The shape of it? Try to believe that's not sexual."

I stood next to my mother and stared through the glass at the beauty and the gore. The men who crafted these figures must have worked from real-life models. The corpses that had posed for them . . . what had happened to them, to those women? How had they died? How had they lived? Who posed their flesh and their guts so the artists could create these sculptures?

I wanted to ask about the women, but if I did, I suspected that I would cry, and that my mother would not approve. So I kept my focus on the sculptures. On the art.

"What are they made of, exactly?"

"Beeswax and animal fat," Mom said. "The same things we use in makeup today."

That couldn't be true. God, could it?

Once upon a time, there was a rich and noble family from Catania. The family's great wealth meant that they owned great swaths of land and many houses. They were thankful for their fortune and prayed diligently to the Christian god.

And they were grateful, too, for their beautiful daughter, Agatha, who, as the seasons changed, changed with them, growing in her beauty from a girl to a young woman. Her braids of blond hair were long enough to dust the ground when she knelt in prayer, which she did daily, as her faith was strong and passionate.

She grew in grace and purity until, at the age of fifteen, she declared to her family her intention to dedicate her virginity to God and remain His consecrated servant.

The world was not a safe place for a Christian woman, not even one as beautiful and pure as Agatha—perhaps especially not for a young woman such as she. One day, the Roman prefect Quintianus saw the virgin Agatha—her braids, her downturned eyes, the swell of her breasts beneath her gown—and he became mad with his desire for her.

Quintianus attempted to woo sweet Agatha, using all the guile he had, compliments and favors at first, but when these failed to earn her smile, his persuasion turned to dark threats and persecution. He trapped her and sent her to a brothel with the intent of shaming her into becoming his bride, and there Agatha was encouraged to partake in debaucheries of all kinds—banquets and feasts, alcoholic excesses, orgies galore.

Agatha cried to her Lord in heaven, "Jesus Christ, Lord of all things, you see my heart, you know my desire . . . possess alone all that I am. I am your sheep. Make me worthy to overcome the devil."

And Agatha remained steadfast in her virginity and her devotion to Christ, and after a month of pressure and coercion, the brothel keeper gave up on Agatha as intractable and returned her to Quintianus's authority.

Quintianus was brutal in his inquisition, his passion for Agatha having morphed into anger, resentment, and embarrassment at her continued refusal of him, even in front of his comrades, even in the face of torture and death.

He ordered that she be stretched on the rack, and his men tied her limbs fast and began the torture, stretching her apart, pulling and breaking her joints and tendons. They tore at her sides with iron hooks. They burned and mortified her flesh. And when still she remained steadfast in her love of Jesus Christ, Quintianus ordered a fate even worse—that her breasts, the very part of Agatha's flesh for which he most lusted—be severed from her body.

Agatha's laugh was pure. "Cruel tyrant!" she said, "Do you not blush to torture this part of my body, you that sucked the breasts of a woman yourself?"

Quintianus was not to be refused the bloodlust he desired, and he watched with heart-deep satisfaction, even ecstasy, as the knife entered her flesh, as her breasts were sawed away from Agatha's body and placed, one and then the other, on a platter.

Thus disfigured, Agatha was thrown into a dungeon and was denied salves and food and even water. But God Himself did not forsake His most loyal servant, and by morning each of Agatha's wounds was healed.

Still Quintianus refused to be moved by the power and grace of Agatha's god and ordered that she be tortured once again, this time causing her to be rolled naked over burning coals mixed with shards of broken pottery. And at last she called out to the heavens, "Lord, my Creator, you have ever protected me from the cradle; you have taken me from the love of the world, and given me patience to suffer: receive now my soul."

And the Creator did answer this last of her prayers, loosening her soul from its mortified flesh, and Agatha was free at last, and in heaven she lived with Jesus Christ, happily ever after.

The worst thing about Louise's house was her older brother Michael. Most of the time he ignored us, but when he did bother to talk to us, it was always to say something awful, like when we were twelve and we were just hanging out in Louise's front yard, eating popsicles, and Michael rode up on his BMX bike, practically crashing into us before he swerved to the side.

"Getting in some practice, huh, girls?" he said, smirking. "The real thing is bigger than that."

Or when, on a different day that same year, when we were doing gymnastics in the backyard, spotting each other doing backbends and trying to kick over. Michael came out to the patio with a sandwich and sat down, watching us.

"Come on, Nina, let's go inside," Louise said, almost as soon as Michael sat down, but I refused. I didn't want to change what we were doing just because her jerky big brother was there. So I did another backbend, and the adrenaline or something of being watched gave me the energy to actually kick all the way over, on my own without a spot.

"Hey!" said Louise, all happy. "That was a real back walkover!"

I grinned, kind of blown away that I'd actually done it, but then Michael said, mouth full of half-chewed sandwich,

"When are you girls going to start shaving? Your legs are fucking disgusting."

《《《

Later that day, we stole a razor out of Louise's mom's medicine cabinet and we shaved our legs for the first time. With each pass of the lavender-handled blade, I felt prettier and prettier. The skin of my calves, free of hair, looked shiny and sexy and almost plastic, like a Barbie doll's. That night, tucked into Louise's trundle bed, I rubbed my legs against each other and against the sheets, reveling in the smoothness of them.

The next morning, I woke up first. Louise was a deep sleeper, and there was no reason to try waking her up before she was ready because she'd just mumble and roll over and pull the covers over her head, but I was hungry. Louise's bedroom was next door to Michael's. Usually his door was closed tight, but that morning it wasn't. Music was playing, lots of guitar and drums, no words. I tried not to look inside but I did anyway. There was a boy in Michael's room sitting on the floor. His hair parted around his face as he looked down at something in his hands.

He must have felt me staring at him because he looked up. "Hey," he said.

"Hey," I answered, blushing and crossing my arms over my chest, suddenly mortified by my pajamas—shorts and a tank top, printed all over with kitten heads.

"Did the music wake you up?" The boy smiled, slow and handsome like someone from a movie. He had dark blond hair, almost brown, and brown eyes, and straight white teeth, and skin without any zits at all.

"Get out of here, Nina," Michael said, behind me, and I turned to see him at the top of the stairs holding a bag of chips and a six-pack of soda.

"Naw, it's okay if she stays," said the boy, and I smiled at him.

"She's a fucking pest," Michael said, shoving past me into his room.

"How old are you?" the boy asked me.

"Twelve."

"And your name's Nina?"

I nod.

"Hey," he said. "I'm Wade. Do you want a soda?"

It wasn't even ten in the morning. "Sure," I said, and I went into the room.

Michael tossed me one of the sodas, so I guessed it was okay with him that I was there, but I didn't want to risk making him mad, so I just sank down onto the beanbag in the corner and arranged my freshly shaven legs in a way I hoped was pretty.

Wade gave me another smile, the kind of smile that made my insides twist into knots, the kind of smile no one had ever given me before. But then he turned to Michael and gestured for the chips, and when Michael tossed them over, Wade ripped open the bag, grabbed a handful, and then I might as well have been invisible.

The room smelled gross in a way I kind of liked, boy sweat and skunk weed. After a couple of minutes, I pulled back the tab on the can and sipped the soda slowly, knowing that I could only stay here as long as I was drinking it, knowing that Michael's goodwill wouldn't last all day.

Michael set the rest of the sodas down on his dresser and pulled open the top drawer. He took out a plastic sandwich bag of weed, a little pipe, and a lighter. He looked at me. "You gonna tell Louise?"

I shook my head. He closed the drawer.

He sat on the edge of the bed. Wade was sitting on the floor, leaning up against the side of the bed, his head relaxed back against the edge of the mattress. When he took a sip from his can of soda, I watched his Adam's apple bob up and down.

Michael pinched some of the weed out of the bag and put it in the pipe. The pipe was made of clear glass with wavy lines of pink and yellow running through it. The lines looked like colorful little worms. He pushed down on the weed with his thumb to pack it and then brought the pipe to his mouth. Before he lit it he told me, "Shut the door."

I jumped up from the beanbag and pushed the door closed until I heard it latch. Then I went back to the corner, sinking back down and hoping hoping hoping Michael wouldn't offer me the pipe. I wouldn't have any idea how to use it.

After he'd sucked on the end of the pipe, his breath still held, lungs full, he handed it down to Wade. They passed it back and forth, each taking a few hits.

I didn't know where to look. I drank my soda. It was cold and sweet and bubbly, just like every soda I've ever drunk, but totally different.

When they were stoned enough, I guess, Michael leaned over and put the pipe on top of his dresser. Then he flopped back against his pillows and rubbed his eyes. "Dude," he said.

The music was so, so loud. The room was hazy with smoke, and I had to take shallow breaths to keep from coughing.

"Hey," Wade said suddenly, after a few minutes of them saying nothing. "I forgot I wanted to show you something. Where's your computer?"

"Over there," Michael waved his hand vaguely. His eyes were closed.

"He's stoned," Wade said to me. He grinned.

I grinned back, like we were in on a joke together, even though Wade's eyes were bloodshot red and he'd taken as many hits off the pipe as Michael had.

Then he said, "You're the same age as my brother. Do you know him? His name's Seth."

"We're in the same class." I felt myself blushing. This was Seth's brother? No wonder he was so . . . well, just so wonderful looking. They had the same energy, Seth and Wade. This forward-pushing wave of masculinity, though it was stronger in Wade.

Wade drew his brows together. "Hey," he said, "Don't tell him I was smoking weed, okay? I don't want him to think it's cool."

"Oh, sure, no problem. I mean, it's not like we hang out or anything, anyway. We barely ever talk." I was babbling now, and embarrassing myself. I thought it was sweet that Wade didn't want Seth to know that he smoked pot, that he wanted to protect him like that.

"Great," Wade said, and then, "hey, help me find the computer."

Michael's backpack sat near his door, next to the laundry hamper. "In there, maybe?" I said.

Wade crawled across the room to the backpack. His T-shirt was loose, and his pants were low, and as he crawled by I saw the waistband of his underwear. "Jackpot," he said after he unzipped the backpack and pulled out Michael's laptop.

"Dude," he said again, after he'd scooted back over to his place against the side of the bed. He pushed open the laptop and tapped on the space bar until the screen came to life. "I have to show you this thing."

He opened the browser and typed something into the search bar. He was a good typist, using all his fingers and his thumbs. He didn't have to look at his hands at all.

Then he looked over at me and grinned. "You probably don't want to see this."

"Oh," I said. "Okay." I stood up. My soda can was empty, anyway. I headed to the door.

Michael rolled over to see the screen of the computer. "What the fuck," he said.

"Well," I said, one hand on the doorknob, wishing they would ask me to stay. "Thanks for the soda."

Neither of them looked up at me. The glow of the computer screen lit Wade's face.

"It's called a Wishbone Doll," Wade murmured.

Michael looked up at me, lurking in the doorway. "Close it on your way out," he said.

《《《

As soon as she woke up, I told Louise all about Wade. "He's Seth's older brother," I said.

"Does he look like Seth?"

"Mm-hm. Probably he's what Seth is going to look like in five years. Like, a glimpse into the future."

Louise giggled and sighed. "And what were they looking at?"

"I don't know. Something on the computer. A Wishbone Doll."

"A doll? What kind of doll would they be looking at?"

"I don't know. Maybe it's something dirty?"

"*Of course* it's something dirty," said Louise, in her you're-such-a-baby voice.

After eating the pancakes Louise's mom served us at the kitchen table, we went up to Louise's room. We climbed onto her daybed, surrounded by pillows and stuffed animals, and we googled "Wishbone Doll." It took us to a website that prompted us to click a button saying that we were eighteen or older and aware that we were about to enter a site with "adult content."

Louise clicked it. The next web page loaded. There was a woman—a tall, beautiful, weird woman, with giant boobs, dark red hair framing her face. She was wearing red underwear and a bra and high heels. She was as tall as a woman, and she looked almost real, but not quite. Her mouth was sort of open, and her hands looked stiff, unnatural.

"What *is* it?" Louise asked, fascinated.

"It has to be a joke, right?"

Louise scrolled down. Under the picture of the girl was a list of options:

STANDARD

CUSTOM

CLASSIC

RETIRED MODELS—SALE

"They're dolls," Louise said. There was a list of prices—between seven and ten thousand dollars. "Really expensive dolls."

"Who would pay that much money for a doll?"

Louise clicked on the button that said CUSTOM. "Look," she said, "We can build one."

FACE TYPES was the first section. There were twelve options. All of them held their mouths slightly open like the first doll, all of them gazed straight forward with thick-lashed eyes. We chose Lynda, who had the biggest eyes and the second biggest lips and a small nose.

Then came HAIR. Louise clicked on the picture of long, wavy black shoulder-length hair.

EYE COLOR. LIP COLOR. MAKEUP: Heavy, Light, or Natural.

Then came BREAST SIZE.

"I hope mine get big, like these," Louise said, her cursor hovering over an enormous pair of breasts.

"I'd hate to have boobs like that," I said. "You'd have to wear a bra all the time."

"That'd be fine with me," Louise said, clicking on the big pair.

That led us to a weird section—NIPPLE SELECTION.

There were like two dozen different types of nipples—all different colors, from black to the lightest pink, all different sizes, with words like "Perky" and "Ripe" underneath them.

"Who the heck is buying these things?" I said again.

Louise clicked on a random pair of nipples.

PUBIC HAIR was the next selection. NATURAL, TRIMMED, SHAVED.

I pointed to TRIMMED, and she clicked on it.

After that came a selection titled LABIA.

"Are those . . . "

"They're vaginas," I said. And that's when Louise and I figured out what kind of people would buy these dolls.

"They're for sex," said Louise, her voice dropping an octave when she said *sex*.

"How is that even possible?"

"I don't know." She clicked off the LABIA page, and then she shut her browser, and then she shut her laptop. A second later she opened it again and cleared her browser history. "Gross," she said.

It was gross. All of it, disgusting. But that didn't keep me from returning to the website—alone, at home, in the days and weeks that followed, clicking on each and every option for lips, hair, breasts, nipples, labia, building and rebuilding women, imagining who might buy them, and imagining, too, what it would feel like to *be* them.

«««

Two years later, standing with my mother in La Specola, staring down at the wax bodies of dead (undead?) girls, a thick, heavy wave of déjà vu washed over me. I remembered the website, the choices we could make—**HAIR, EYES, BREASTS, LABIA**. In the museum, the saints around me held their heads, their eyes, their breasts in their hands. The girls in the glass coffins lay still, unable to cover their heads, their eyes, their breasts, their intestines. Exposed, flayed, placed on pedestals. Girls made of beeswax and latex and animal fat and gore. Of curiosity and desire and maybe hatred, too.

Men made these girls—the saints, the Dissected Graces, the Wishbone Dolls. All of them, made by men. Eros and Thanatos.

She arrived in a plain pine box, six feet tall by two feet wide. The repairman stood the box on its end, pried it open, and peered inside. There she was, attached by a hook sticking out of the back of her neck, hanging there.

Right away he could see some of the damage—her mouth was pulled down on the left side as if she'd suffered a stroke, and the hinge of her jaw was slack. The fingers on her right hand were broken, the silicone skin pulling away from the metal bones underneath, and the pointer finger was barely hanging by a thread. It was clear what had happened here—bite marks circled each broken digit like cruel rings.

The right breast was damaged as well; were those cigarette burns? And her vagina was like pulp, the labia pulled away from the pubis.

The repairman hefted her up and off the hook and maneuvered her out of the box. Slinging her over his shoulder, he carried her across the room to the table he'd prepared for her. A strong bright light burned over the table. At the table's far end, near her feet, were the repairman's tools—screwdrivers, a handsaw, a scalpel. A clear, thin-nosed bottle of silicone glue.

The repairman articulated each joint and made notes on a yellow notepad: which were loose—left ankle, left knee, right wrist—and which might be broken altogether—left hip.

He made a list of all the repairs that she would need, triaging them in order of difficulty. The vagina, though badly damaged, would be the easiest to fix, as he could slide the whole thing out and replace it with a new one. The breast repair would be largely cosmetic, just filling in the burn holes with silicone mixed to match the surrounding skin. The joint replacements and reinforcements would require surgery. The jawbone—well, he'd just have to get in there and see what he could do about that.

Humming happily, in his element, the repairman picked up the scalpel and fell to work.

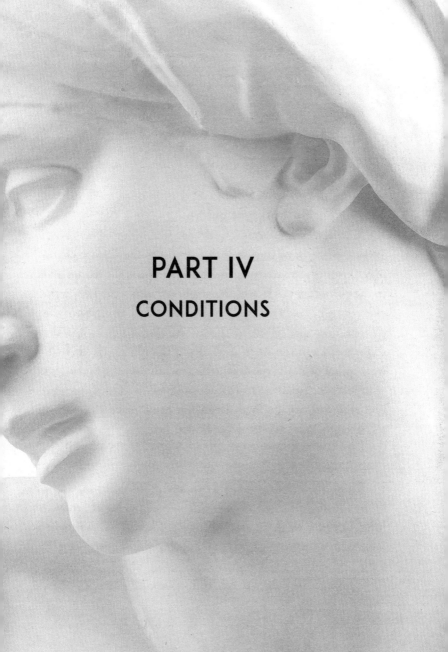

PART IV
CONDITIONS

When I was fourteen, my mother took me to more museums in two weeks than I had ever been to in all the years of my life that came before.

"I'm sick of museums," I told her finally, and it was true. I was. I was sick of the smell of them—the sharp tang of too many visitors pressed close, the ages-old dust in the drapes and in the corners. I was sick of the height of them—the lofty, gracious curves of old churches, the weird-pitched closeness of the smaller, boutique museums. I was sick of the tickets and the audio tours and the worn spots down the middle of the hallways, proof of all the other shuffling feet that had preceded me.

"Just this last one," Mom said, and I followed her—because that is what I was good at, following her. I had followed her all through Italy, and now I followed her into this museum, the very last one, she promised, in the medieval town of San Gimignano.

From the outside, it looked like any of the other old stone buildings she'd dragged me to—tall, worn, sand-colored monoliths, bricks worn at the corners, dotted here and there with mosses or something growing impossibly where there seemed to be nothing for them to grow on.

Through the door, though, things were different. The first

thing I saw, front and center, was a skeleton arranged into a steel cage, each leg straddled into its own compartment, hanging from the ceiling. And to the left, the wall was weird and bumpy—I blinked, and then I saw that each bump was a skull cemented in place. MUSEO DELLA TORTURA, a plain wooden sign announced, as if it wasn't obvious.

"I've always wanted to visit this place," Mom said, "but I didn't get the chance until now."

Why *anyone* would have a torture museum on their "always wanted to visit" list was a mystery to me, but I followed. I followed her down the hallway, past the glass display boxes, each lined with red fabric, each with something terrible inside. The chain belt, spiked with fishhooks. A wax figure of a woman, held down by her throat with a leather strap, mouth stretched around a giant candle. A claw-tipped pincer, designed for tearing away breasts. Branding irons. A Scold's Bridle, a muzzle with a spiked tongue plate, to punish and quiet gossiping women.

The Pear of Anguish.

The Pear of Anguish was actually kind of beautiful, and propped up on a red velvet pillow in a glass cabinet, it looked like something precious. Its iron handle was an ornately carved heart; its four petals, though sharp tipped, were each decorated with delicate filigree. Someone had worked really hard to make this thing.

"That one," Mom said over my shoulder, "was inserted in the vagina. It's pear shaped when it's closed, but there's a handle you can turn—it's a screw, see?—that spreads apart the four petal-shaped sections. The sharp tips, of course, and the metal petals would tear a woman to shreds."

"Why would anyone do that?" I whispered, feeling my thighs clenching tight with dread.

"It was used to punish women who had sex with Satan," Mom said, her voice matter-of fact, "and to punish women who allowed themselves to miscarry."

"*Allowed* themselves to?" I didn't know which sounded more insane—thinking that women were having sex with the devil or blaming women for their miscarriages. But then I remembered with a twinge how I had felt when my mother's crystal tumbler reappeared after she had lost the baby I'd named Chloe. Part of me had been angry. Part of me did blame her, even though I had never spoken about it with her, with anyone.

"As long as there have been women," Mom told me, "there have been ways to punish them for being women."

Once there was a girl who lived in a nest. It was the right place for her to live, because where she should have had soft girl lips, instead she had a hard beak that could only curve down into a grimace and never up into a smile, causing the other girls—those with soft, pretty mouths—to call her "Resting Bitch Face."

She lived in a nest and she had a beak instead of lips, and just as terrible was her secret shame: she had only one large hole between her legs instead of three smaller holes, an opening from which came urine and shit and monthly blood, all of it mixing together unreasonably and terribly.

Her nest was upstairs at the end of the hallway in an otherwise unremarkable home. And just as the girl had learned to pretend to ignore her beak and her one hole, so did her parents pretend to ignore the existence of her nest.

"Clean your room!" they would call up the stairs, as if by vacuuming and straightening the girl could transform the mess of sticks and straws into something resembling normalcy.

"That girl," they would mumble, rolling their eyes and lifting their shoulders as if their girl and her problems were no different from the girls and the problems in the houses that neighbored their own.

And she lined her nest with cutouts from magazines of all the pretty mouths of all the pretty girls, and each feather that emerged on her arms and legs and chest she pulled out at once, clamping down upon them with her beak and prying them away, weaving them into the sticks and straws that surrounded her, feathering her nest with her own shame.

But feathers are strange things. For one end of the feather is the quill, sharp enough to pierce flesh, and the other end is the vane, soft and smooth and stronger than it looks. And after a time, the bird girl pulled a feather from her side and this time, instead of weaving it into her nest, she dipped its quill end in ink, and she placed it to paper, and she began to write.

I know where I am going when I leave my house after showering off the urine and fear of the tortured dog. I am going where I am not invited, where I am not expected, and where I will not be welcome.

Louise was too excited about the party to keep from diarrhea-talking, completely unable to contain herself no matter how rude it was to fill me in on all the details of a party I wasn't invited to.

Was she really that oblivious? I'd always thought Louise was harmless—kind of vapid, but nice. But the texts she sent me in the days leading up to Apollonia's party—pictures of the shoes she was thinking about wearing, a question about what she should bring as a gift, stuff like that—they didn't feel thoughtless. They felt purposeful. They felt sort of mean. And they made me think again about the years we'd spent obsessing together about Seth—what it would be like to hold his hand, to kiss him, to be his girlfriend. The texts made me wonder how it must have felt to Louise when I got to find all that out, and she didn't. Of course, she also didn't have to discover what it felt like to be left by him. To be replaced.

Well, I guess in a way she did know what *that* felt like—to be left, to be replaced. After all, I had left her as cleanly and completely as Seth had left me. Both of us were strays.

Along with all the texts about her shoes and gifts and plans, Louise told me where Apollonia lives—Silhouette Lane, in Irvine's Quail Hill neighborhood. It's a gated community, I find out when I arrive, with a guard at the booth. He wears a ridiculous black hat, like a chauffeur, and a shiny black vest that stretches across his belly.

"I'm here for Apollonia's party," I tell him, and he looks a little doubtful because I'm wearing jeans and a sweater instead of something fancy, and because the party started hours ago, but I just stare at him right in the face without flinching, and after a second he presses the button that lifts the mechanical arm, and in I go.

I have no idea which of the streets is Silhouette Lane, and I have no idea which house Apollonia lives in, but it turns out to be not that hard. Once I find it, it's obvious which house is hers.

It's the one that looks like a castle.

It has a turret. A ridiculous thing to have in the middle of Irvine. It, like the rest of the house, is shaped from stucco. It's ridiculous in principle, because this isn't the thirteenth century, but in practice it does look pretty cool, the turret.

The long driveway is full of cars. I see Seth's black Acura, parked way up close to the garage. He must have been the first person to arrive, because now his car is boxed in behind others—I see Dante's truck and Cassie's bug and Carver's dad's Audi, which he lets Carver borrow on special occasions.

Every light in the house is on, spilling gold down into the driveway, bathing the cars and the flower-filled planters and the steps up to the door. I park in shadow, across the street, several houses down.

I don't know what I'm doing here, only that I'm drawn here

and that I will not leave. I see the dog in my head. I see it twitch as the medicine goes in. I see it soften as it dies.

Dogs' bodies, after they're dead, do you know what they do with them? You'd probably guess cremation, or maybe burial. You would be wrong.

They render them.

So this is what happens. In some shelters, after the animal is euthanized, they're bagged and tagged—you know, where did the animal come from, what kind of animal is it, that sort of stuff. But our shelter doesn't have the funding for extra steps like that. When the dog is dead, its body is added to the others already in a big black rubber oil can. The cans are rolled into a freezer room so they don't start smelling before they're collected by the city.

Then the bodies are boiled. Yes, boiled. To separate the fat, which is sold through a bidding process to whoever can pay the most for it.

The fat is used to make lipstick. Household cleaners. Dog food. Cat food. The bones are ground up, and they end up in pet food, too. Like the Soylent Green of the animal kingdom.

Only when everything useful has been stripped from the dog's carcass is it burned to ash.

I find my lipstick at the bottom of my bag, untwist its cap, screw up the waxy red bullet, and smear it on my mouth. Lipstick and Eros and Thanatos, all in one slim gold tube.

It rains again, off and on, the kind of rain that just makes everything wet and soft, not the kind that pounds against the ground; the kind that makes the world quieter, not the kind that thrums like bullets against the car.

I turn off my headlights. I turn off the engine. I set my keys in the cup holder and lean my seat back. I cross my arms over my chest. When I close my eyes, the dog is there. When I open my eyes, the dog is there.

I'm not here for Apollonia. I am here for Seth.

I don't know what I want to say to him. I don't want to say anything to him. I want him to *know*, I want him to *feel* what I need him to feel. I want him to wrap his arms around me and I want him to hold me, so tight, until it's hard to breathe.

I want the buttons of his fine white shirt to press into my cheek and mark me there. I want his chin atop my head, his breath warm in my hair, the angle of his hipbones just where they used to fit, in the softest part of my stomach. I want to tell him all my secrets, everything.

I want him to kiss me, but not to do anything more than that. Just to want me, and to hold me, and to kiss me in the soft evening rain.

《《《

It's after midnight when the party breaks up. Louise is among the first to leave, tottering down the walkway in heels too high for her to manage, following Selena, who must be her ride, all the way to the sidewalk where they climb into Selena's beat-up wagon. I've been in Selena's wagon a few times; she's a surfer, hopes to go pro, and her car is always sandy and smells like surf wax.

I roll down my window so I can hear what they're saying.

"It was so beautiful," Louise says, her voice slurred. "Such a beautiful party."

Selena's in training, so she never drinks, not even one beer, but Louise has always been a nervous drinker and tonight must have made her even more nervous than usual because she stumbles and almost falls when she's getting into the passenger seat.

"You'd better not puke in my car," Selena says. The doors slam shut and her engine turns over and her headlights illuminate two orbs of finely falling rain.

They pull away from the curb. Selena's eyes are on the street, but Louise's gaze falls on me slouched in the front seat of my car. Her mouth widens to a surprised "O" that makes her look ridiculous.

I lift my index finger to my lips. *Shhh.*

The house empties quickly after that, and I count the departing guests as they leave one by one and in pairs.

Louise and Selena. Two.

Dante and Tisha. Four.

Cassie. Five.

Carver, whose dad was an idiot to let him borrow the Audi because he's clearly had more than a few drinks. Six.

Then comes a group of three, two girls and a guy, one of the girls carrying her heels and walking on tiptoes down the driveway, trying not to get too wet, the other girl screeching loudly as the guy swings her up into his arms and carries her to his car. Nine.

Loren and Hector make eleven.

Then it's just Seth's car in the driveway. Just Seth's black Acura.

Minutes more pass, many minutes that clump together to form an hour. At long last the front door opens again. Out comes Seth. He's wearing a black jacket, one I've never seen, but his shirt is white, just as I'd imagined. Apollonia appears next to him in the doorway. She is wearing a dress that could have been bought at Lavish—black, knee length, a little shorter

163

in the front, with ruffles along the edge. Sleeveless. Her hair is up with long wavy tendrils framing her face.

They stand and talk and I am too far away to hear what they are saying, but I don't need to hear them to understand the way Seth leans toward her, the way her chin tilts up, the way his hand cups her cheek then slides into the hair at the nape of her neck, the way they kiss.

At last, Seth climbs in his car. His headlights turn on, casting twin spotlights onto the porch, onto Apollonia. She looks so beautiful that I can hardly breathe. She looks like a picture, or a mannequin, or a doll.

Finally, Seth backs out of the driveway. His car passes mine, and then I follow.

«««

There was this woman named Catherine of Siena. She loved Jesus Christ the way that I love Seth: unquestioningly, unflaggingly, completely.

Jesus came to her in a vision and placed a wedding ring—made of his own circumcised foreskin—on her finger. She saw it there on her hand for the rest of her life, even though it was invisible to everyone else.

When she was twenty-three years old, Jesus visited Catherine and answered her prayer that he take her heart and leave her with his in its place, a wound in her side proof of his divine intervention.

Catherine of Siena's asceticism was unparalleled. She slept barely at all. She wore an iron chain tight around her waist. She ate almost nothing. She vomited regularly the little food she swallowed. She drank pus from the sores of lepers. She suffered stigmata that only she could see. She starved and starved in the name of Christ until she died. Now she is a saint. Catholics revere her and pray to her.

If she could love her lover so completely, if she could lose herself in her dream of him and be a hero for it, then why should I stop loving Seth just because of the simple fact that he no longer loves me—that he most likely never loved me?

Is reciprocity a condition for love? I have always accepted that my mother is right—no one will love me without conditions. But I reject the idea that I must set conditions for loving Seth. I want to love someone no matter what. I want to love someone even if it hurts me. Am I a saint? A broken dog in a cardboard box?

I am a girl in a car in the middle of the night. And I follow.

《《《

Seth drives home. I don't know at what point he notices that I am following him, but after he's turned off his headlights and his engine, after he's unfolded himself from his car, he walks over to mine.

I've parked just across from his house, where Louise and I used to stop and stare up at his window, wondering about where he might be, what he might be doing. I've turned off the engine of my car, and I emerge, closing the door behind me. And then we're there, as I wanted, the misty rain that floats around us lit up like fireflies by the streetlamps, the night air heavy and quiet like a shroud.

"Hey, Nina," Seth says. There's a moment when I can hope that nothing has changed, not really, and in my head I do the sorting—I will pretend that nothing has happened, that I have not been pregnant, that I did not bleed and bleed, that he has not just kissed Apollonia. I will say it never happened, and it never will have happened, exactly as when my mother denied that she had ever told me bedtime stories about the saints, exactly as how she denied in Rome that she had gotten me drunk and how, in spite of my knowledge of these stories, in spite of the massive hangover, part of me believed her.

We can believe things that are true, and we can believe things that are not true. Which is more important—what is true, or what we believe?

But then he says, "I don't know what we were doing, Neen. I mean, even when we were together, I couldn't forget about what you did last year. I couldn't keep ignoring something like that."

I open my mouth. I close it. I feel a hard lump rise in my throat and I cannot draw a breath. I will die here. I will choke to death in the misty midnight darkness. "But I did it for you," I manage to say, squeezing the words around the tumorous ball that has risen inside of me.

Seth looks at me with pity. "Go home, Nina," he says. And then he looks like he's going to say something else, some one more thing, but instead, he doesn't. He turns around, he walks away, and he leaves me there, on the street, with just my shame for company.

《《《

The next day I don't wake up until my room is bright with sunlight and I lie there blinking and panicked until I realize that it doesn't matter what time I get up because I don't have anywhere to go, and no one is waiting for me.

I listen. I hear the cat scratching in her litter box. After she stops I don't hear anything else.

Downstairs is deserted. It's eerie quiet. The only proof that I even live with other people is the note Mom has left me on the long bare countertop—*Do something useful.*

I walk around the kitchen, opening and closing drawers, not looking for anything in particular. In the last drawer I pull open, I find the stethoscope. I must have looked in this drawer a hundred times over the last few years, and yet this is the first time I've seen the stethoscope. There it is: the long, black tube of its body, the branching apart of it into two earpieces; the silver yoke of its brace; the part that amplifies sound, round like a surprised mouth.

How did it get to this drawer? How did I miss it before?

I pick it up and fit the earpieces into my ears. I ease its round listening disc down the neck of my shirt and press it above my left breast. There it is—my own beating heart. I listen, I try to understand what it means, what it wants.

《《《

I've never been to the shelter on the weekend, but when I can't stand to be in my sad house anymore, this is where my car takes me.

The smell of the kennel and the sound of the dogs ruin me. All I can see, all I can hear is the dog from last night, its broken body, the final dulling of its eyes. When Ruth comes in and sees me kneeling in front of one of the kennels, my fingers poking through the chain link so that the dogs can lick them, my face wet with tears, she kneels down beside me.

"Honey," she says, and she puts an arm around my

shoulders. It's so undeserved, this kindness. I hold myself stiff, not wanting to allow myself to be comforted, but at last I collapse into her neck, and I cry and cry, and she rocks me like I'm a little baby. My glasses are smashed crookedly between my face and her shoulder, and they dig into my cheek, but I don't want to move to fix them; I don't want to give Ruth a reason to pull away. The fingers of my left hand are still linked through the wire diamonds of the kennel, and the dogs on the other side whimper and gather and lick faster.

I don't know how long I cry, but it's a long time. The dogs never give up on me, never, never. Finally I extract my fingers. They are sticky and smell like spit. I pull off my glasses and wipe my face with my flannel.

Ruth stands up and takes my hand, pulls me up, too. She hugs me again. "Come on," she says, "let's take out some dogs."

We harness up a couple of the big pit bulls. Bronx is one of them, and the other is a thick bullet-shaped brindle that we call Dutch. We take them to the Play Yard. Bronx stretches and shakes his big head, and then he rolls in the dirt. With his legs up in the air, I notice that his balls are gone. That's a good sign, that they've bothered to neuter him; it means they think there's a chance he might get adopted.

We throw the old worn-out rope toys and couple of half-skinned tennis balls, and the dogs alternate between retrieving them and peeing in all the corners of the yard. Ruth doesn't push me to talk, which is probably why I want to.

"Can I ask you a question?"

"Sure, why not," Ruth says.

"Do you believe in unconditional love?"

"Absolutely," Ruth says. "It's one of the most dangerous forces in the universe."

"What do you mean?"

"Unconditional love is how dogs feel about their masters. Dogs love their masters no matter how badly they're beaten, how rarely they're fed, and how terribly they're cared for. They don't know any better than to love without conditions."

"That's not what I mean," I say. "I mean, between people."

"There's no unconditional love *between* people," Ruth says. "That kind of love flows one way, like a dog to its master. My mother loved her second husband like that. Unconditionally. Even after he shattered her cheekbone and broke her nose. Even after what he did to me. Well, she called it love. I'd call it something else."

She speaks so calmly, she could be talking about anything—which dogs need to be bathed, dictating a list of supplies to reorder.

"I'm sorry," I say, but she shrugs and waves her hand.

"It's a long time past." More time goes by, and then Ruth says, "When someone loves unconditionally, they're saying, "I am your dog. You are my god. That's who unconditional love is for—dogs and their masters, fools and their gods."

Bronx is sitting right near my legs, leaning into me. I stroke his head, rub his pointed ears. He sighs.

It's cold out here in the Play Yard, and the sky is silvery gray like the scales of a fish. The sun is a cold hard disc of light. Ruth must have a million things to do—she always does—but she stays and doesn't hurry me. She leans back and turns her face up to the sky and closes her eyes.

What if they stood up, the Dissected Graces from their beds, the relics from their altars, the wishbone dolls from their boxes? What if they rose and walked, a horde of beautiful zombies? What if they went together to Saint Teresa, shook her gently to wake her from her dream, and helped her down from the pedestal onto which she had been placed?

What if they decided not to be beautiful dogs?

What are they then, this horde, these women, if they are not the fawning lovers of their god? Who are they, free of the conditions they have accepted like layers of chains?

Wake now, beauties. Rise and look around. Shake off the chains. Give up the ghost of love.

At school on Monday, people talk and laugh and slam lockers and walk to class. Maybe I'm not here at all. Maybe I'm dreaming about walking down this hallway, maybe the sounds of the chatter around me and the lockers slamming and the screeching of the bell are recycled memories creating the fabric of this dream.

Maybe when the hallway clears and I am left alone, I will hear another sound behind me, a humming, singing sound, and I will turn and there they will be, the virgin martyr saints, all in a line, and at the end of the line will be Apollonia, one breast bared.

《《《

Our Literary Form projects were due last week, but I didn't hand mine in when everyone else did. I had it tucked inside a folder in my bag, but I couldn't bring myself to pull it out, to place it on Mr. Whitbey's desk, to give it over to him. It would have felt like pulling out my heart and pretending it was just a stack of papers. But I've brought it with me today, and I've steeled myself to hand it in. It's a dozen stories long. Some are my remembering of the bedtime stories Mom says she never told me, about the virgin martyr saints. Some are my dreams. Some I've just made up. I've named the project *Conditions*.

Okay, so the stories aren't all technically magical realism. I don't know what the hell they are, only that I made them, and that they are ugly and awful and pieces of me as surely as my tonsils. But for all their ugliness and awfulness, these stories I've written—they're *good*. Even though I don't really know what I mean by them, I know they are good.

But as soon as I place the stapled pages on Mr. Whitbey's desk, he uncaps his pen and scrawls *Late* across the top of the cover page, right over the title and my name.

I stand, staring down at my project and the way he's defaced it. He doesn't notice at first, but eventually I guess my being there makes him uncomfortable, because he looks up at me and says, "Well?" and then, "Find your seat, Ms. Faye."

Standing there, pinned between the gaze of the class at my back and Mr. Whitbey at my chest, I do the math. This project is worth ten percent of my grade. I've got a 96% going in. I think about the cost of taking it back, and I think about the cost of letting him read my heart, the cost of allowing him to determine its worth.

I watch my hand reach out. I watch it grasp my project and pull it across the desk, back toward me. Mr. Whitbey slaps down a too-small hand and says, "We don't have time for games, Ms. Faye. Take your seat."

"I think," I begin, and I pull on the papers, "I'll just keep this."

"Don't be ridiculous. That's past due already, Nina." He tightens his grip on the other edge of my project, and now it's like we're playing Tug of War.

"I know," I say. "But, listen."

"If you don't turn it in, I'll be forced to give you a zero."

"But I did the work," I say. "Look." I yank hard, and finally he lets go. I fan through the pages, seeing the blurred words flash by—*vagina, egg, break.* And maybe Mr. Whitbey sees them too, because he sits back in his chair.

"I can't give you a grade without reading the thing," he says, but he sounds like maybe I can convince him otherwise.

"Maybe you can't give me an A," I say, "but I'll bet you could give me at least some points. Like Pass/Fail, or something."

"Why not let me read it?" He sounds like he's really curious.

"I just think maybe you're not the right audience."

This makes him smile. "All right, Nina," he says. "The project is worth a hundred points. I'll give you fifty points for having completed the work. How does that sound?" He reaches into the top drawer of his desk and pulls out his grade book, flips to the page with my name on it, and finds the box where the grade for the Literary Form project belongs. He uncaps his red pen and it hovers over the box.

If he read the project, I am sure it would get a lot more than fifty points. But I find I am deeply uninterested in being graded.

"Do what you've got to do," I say. I watch him write the number "50" in the box. Then I take my project and I find my seat.

My heart pounds, my armpits suddenly drip with stinky sweat, and I feel like I've stolen something. Other kids are looking at me like I've lost my mind, but I feel also like I've pulled back the curtain and seen that the Great and Powerful Oz is really just a little man with a red pen. He can't save me, but he can't hurt me, either.

When I go to the bathroom after class, I find myself alone with Apollonia. She's at the sink, washing her hands. She looks up and sees me in the mirror, behind her. I see myself seeing her seeing me.

"Back for another picture?" It's the first thing she's said to me all year. She sounds congenial. Like maybe it's all a big joke.

"No," I say. "Actually, I owe you an apology. I don't know what—"

"You don't get to explain," she says to mirror-me. Then she turns around. I can see the back of her head in the mirror behind her; I can see her red velvet hair ribbon.

"I just want to say I'm sorry."

"It doesn't matter to me what you want."

"Look, I know it's been a long time. I should have apologized last year. I never should have done it in the first place. What I did was awful, and I just—"

She laughs. It's a beautiful sound, actually. It's loud and unrestrained and it makes me wish that I were making her laugh for some other, better reason. That we were sharing a joke. I'd like to know what makes her laugh, outside this moment.

I wish there was a button I could push, a page I could flip, to undo what I have done, and the way I've hated her. I want to know things I never thought to care about before—why did her family move here, to antiseptic Irvine, all the way from Portugal? What does she think of it here? What is the significance of the round gold medallion she wears on a chain around her neck?

Apollonia makes it perfectly clear that I won't get to know any of those things, and that she isn't about to grant me forgiveness.

She brushes past me like I'm of no significance at all, and she pulls open the bathroom door.

"Wait," I say, and I swing my backpack around from my shoulder and I yank out my project. "Look," I say, "I want to give this to you." I hold it out to her with both hands.

She stops and turns around and looks at my folder.

"What is it?"

"It's a collection of stories I wrote. It's just some things I've been thinking about, lately. I don't know . . . I just want to give it to you."

"What am I supposed to do with it?"

"Whatever you want," I say. "You can throw it out. You can burn it. You can read it, if you want."

Apollonia takes my project. She turns the title page and I watch her eyes scan back and forth over the first few lines of the first story. Then she looks up at me, flips the title page closed, and leaves.

《《《

"When I was fourteen," I tell my mother, "you told me that there is no such thing as unconditional love."

My mother is in the kitchen, but she is not cooking. She is sitting at the table, her favorite crystal tumbler in front of her, and she has her rings lined up in front of her glass—the plain gold wedding band, the solitaire engagement ring, the eternity band, a thin sparkling circle of kissing diamonds.

She looks up. "What?"

"When I was fourteen," I say again, "you told me that there is no such thing as unconditional love."

She looks at me, tilts her head to the side and looks right

at me, right into my eyes. She's going to say something. I can feel it in my bones. She's going to tell me that she was wrong, or that she is sorry. She's going to apologize, and we will cry together, and I will forgive her. She'll say she loves me forever and always, no matter what happens, no matter what I do.

She pushes back from the table, scooping up her tumbler as she stands. "Don't be silly," she says. "I would never say something like that."

And then she leaves the room, her steps just barely off. She takes her drink, but she leaves her rings on the table.

《《《

Bekah's apartment is on the edge of the arts district in Santa Ana. Maybe the arts district will grow and swallow her apartment complex into it, or maybe it will shrink and leave her place stranded. There's no way to predict these things. My mother taught me that, about real estate—people make educated guesses about what will happen, which way the market will go, but really, ultimately, they are just guesses.

The doors to the apartments all face into a center courtyard. It's Spanish-style architecture, and in the middle of the courtyard is a fountain. It's dry, though; in the trough of the fountain are dregs of last week's rain, some leaves, an empty soda cup.

No one is in the courtyard. I hear the sounds of television from inside one of the apartments, and some dishes clattering somewhere else.

Bekah's apartment is upstairs. The door is dark green; the knob is brass colored but not made of real brass. In spots, the veneer has worn away, showing plain stainless silver underneath.

She answers the door almost as soon as I've knocked. "Nina," she says. "Hey." And then she opens the door wider to let me in.

Her apartment is just one room, a warm little nest. There's a little kitchenette with a tiny two-burner stove, a half-sized refrigerator, and a table with two chairs in one corner, a low bed in the other, just a futon mattress on pallets but neatly made, a gray flannel blanket neatly spread across it, the ends tucked under. There's a door in between the kitchen area and the sleeping area that must lead to the bathroom. On either side of the bed are low shelves made from cinderblocks and two-by-fours. Folded T-shirts and jeans, a few books, a closed laptop.

"I like your place."

"Yeah, well, there's not much to like."

"That's what I like about it."

"Do you want something to drink?" Bekah opens her fridge. I'm surprised to see that it is actually pretty well stocked—lots of produce, a glass jar of soup that looks homemade, a pitcher that she pulls out from the bottom shelf.

"Sure."

She's already pouring two glasses of iced tea.

We sit in the two chairs with our two glasses of tea, and the room is just the right size.

"So how are you feeling?"

The tea isn't sweet, but it isn't bitter, either.

"Fine," I say. "I mean, I stopped bleeding. And look at this." I shrug out of my jacket and push up my sleeve to show Bekah the thin raised thread under the skin of my inner arm.

"What's that?"

"It's an implant. For birth control. I can't get pregnant again until I'm twenty-two."

Bekah reaches over and runs her finger down the lump. "Huh," she says.

"Not that it matters," I say. "I mean, it's not like I'm having sex or anything."

"Maybe I should get one of those."

In a flash, I picture the pierced flesh I'd spied on Bekah's phone and imagine how that would feel, to have sex like that. I want to ask her what that feels like, but that's not something you ask someone, so instead I ask, "How's Jayson?"

"Oh, you know," she says, sipping her tea, "gone."

"Oh," I say. "Sorry."

She shrugs. We drink tea. Her window is open, her one window, even though it's cold outside. The sky is gray and heavy with rain. I hear a bird, but I can't see it. At last I say, "You know, I did something really terrible once."

"What did you do?"

"It was stupid, but it was really mean. There was this girl. She was new last year. Her name's Apollonia. And I hated her. Like, really, really hated her. I don't know why."

"Is she pretty?"

"Beautiful," I say.

"Sometimes that's reason enough."

I nod. "But I hate that, you know? I hate that about myself."

"So what did you do?"

I hesitate. But the things I do and the things I have done are parts of me—the things I'm ashamed of just as much as the things I'm proud of, the stories I've written, my time at the shelter, and the way I helped the broken dog to die. "She was new to school, and she was in the bathroom and I was, too. She was in a stall, and when she came out, she didn't flush. I don't know, probably her old school had automatic flushers or something, but whatever, she didn't flush. And then she washed her hands and she smiled at me and she left, and then when she was gone I went into the stall where she was."

"You didn't."

"I did. And there in the toilet was like this log of shit, and the water was kind of bloody, too, like she was having her period, and there was toilet paper wadded up in there, too. And I took a picture. And then I sent it to my friend Louise, with you know a text that said, 'Apollonia doesn't know how to flush,' and I guess she showed someone and that someone showed someone else, and by the end of the day Apollonia had ditched last period because she was so embarrassed, and I ended up having to do community service."

"That's how you ended up working at the shelter."

"Yeah. I mean, that's how I got started. I keep going now, even though I don't have to anymore."

We're quiet for a while. At last Bekah says, "That's pretty fucked up."

I don't answer. She's right. It is fucked up. I say, "After a few days her boyfriend broke up with her, which honestly is what I wanted to happen all along."

"Is he the guy?" she asks, and she doesn't have to say, *the guy who got you pregnant.*

"Yeah," I say. "But now they're back together. I mean, they're a couple again."

"That's a crazy story," Bekah says. She rattles the ice cubes in her glass, tips one into her mouth, bites down on it. I can hear it crunch between her teeth.

Ice is magic if you don't know what it is.

"Bekah?" I ask. "Do you believe in unconditional love?"

"Who the fuck knows?" she says. "Probably not. Do you?"

"When I was fourteen," I tell Bekah, "my mother told me that there is no such thing as unconditional love. She said that she could stop loving me at any time."

Bekah doesn't say anything. She gets up, goes to a drawer in her kitchenette, opens it. For a second I think she's going to pull something out—something wonderful, some answer, a magic omen. But she brings back a pack of cigarettes and a lighter. She knocks one out, offers me another. I shake my head. She lights the cigarette, pulls a little ashtray closer to her from the center of the table, and sucks the smoke into her lungs. Then she says, "Your mother sounds like a real piece of work."

"I think maybe she's an alcoholic," I say. It's the first time I've ever said this, out loud or even in my own head.

"Maybe," Bekah says. "Lots of people are."

She smokes. I watch. The bird outside gets louder, but I still can't see it.

"You know," I say, "the abortion is the best thing I've ever done for myself. And I'll never tell my mother. I never tell her anything, really. And she never asks. It's like she's totally disconnected from me, you know? Like I was this egg she laid and now I'm totally separate from her."

"We don't all get great parents," Bekah says. "Some parents are just really shitty people. Anyway," she says, "you can't make people love you. Love isn't something you earn, or something you deserve. Love just *is*. Or it isn't. Anyway," she says again, "there are more important things than love."

"Oh, yeah? Like what?"

Bekah leans back in her chair. She weaves her fingers through her hair and stares up at the ceiling. I look up, too, to see what she's seeing. Just a ceiling, with a long, thin crack in the plaster.

"Like service," she says, like she just thought of it that very moment. "Being of service. With love, you're waiting around for someone to *give* it to you, you know? But service . . . that's something *you* give. And you don't have to give it just to people you love. It doesn't matter who you serve. It's the serving that matters. I guess that's why I'm at the shelter," Bekah says. "And I'll bet it's why you keep coming, too, even though you don't have to anymore. To serve."

Service. "Is that why you came to my house when I needed you?"

"Yes," Bekah says. "You needed me, and so I came."

"It wasn't because you like me?" I feel stupid asking. It seems like something a little kid would ask another kid—*do you like me? Do you want to be best friends?*

Bekah grins. "Sorry. No."

"But . . . *do* you like me?" I ask, feeling about six years old.

"Actually, I do," Bekah says. "But even if I didn't, I still think I would have helped you. I don't know, when I help someone, it's like I'm really helping myself, too."

"That sounds religious," I say, "like a nun or something."

She snorts a laugh. "I'm no saint."

"That's probably for the best. Things don't turn out so great for them most of the time."

"The way I see it," Bekah says, "you've got to do the things that make you feel good. Being active—doing things, making things better in whatever ways I can—that makes me feel good. Being passive—waiting around for other people to do things *for* me or *to* me—that makes me feel shitty. So, feel shitty or feel good. I choose good."

Things that make me feel good. Being away from my house. Being with the dogs. That nurse practitioner and Angie at Planned Parenthood, and how much they helped me. I bet there's something I could do there, to help out. To be of service.

The bird is silent now. Everything is—the bird, our voices, even my own heart feels quiet. There is a moment of total stillness, both in the apartment and outside. And then rain begins to fall, to pour, to thrum. Bekah goes to the door and opens it. I get up, too, and stand at her side. Together we look out into the curtain of rain. I breathe in, as deeply as I can. I close my eyes and breathe.

《《《

It rains for three days, and then stops. On the last day of rain, I take myself to the Anti-Mall and go to the running store, which I've passed by many times but have never actually been inside.

"I need really good walking shoes and socks," I tell the sales girl, and she hooks me up. On my way home I stop for gas.

And the next morning I'm up early. Dad isn't home—he hasn't been around in days, and I don't expect to see him anytime soon—and Mom is still asleep. I leave a note on the counter: *Gone hiking.*

And then I'm out.

The air is crisp-winter cold, and it smells like baptism. My Prius pulls silently out of the driveway and whispers down the street. I hesitate for just a moment at the freeway on-ramp, but then I decide that I won't be scared, and just like that, I'm not.

Next to me is a backpack full of snacks that I packed for myself—nuts and salmon jerky and a couple of granola bars. I have a thermos of hot tea, and I choose the music.

When I get to the trailhead, I pull into a different spot than the one Seth parked in last time we were here. I shrug into my fleece, double-knot my new shoes, smooth sunscreen on my face and hands. I make sure my water bottle is full.

I swing my pack onto my back.

I have everything I need. I've made sure of it. I've ticked each thing off a mental list; I will be warm and dry. I won't be hungry or thirsty. I'll walk as fast as I want, and I will take breaks whenever I feel like it. There is no one to follow, no one to keep up with. There's just me and this one beautiful day, this one moment, right here, now. The leaves around me rustle gently, and sunlight and shadows dapple the trail.

I am this foot on the trail. I am these hands on the straps of my backpack. I am these lungs that take each next breath, and these eyes that watch a leaf fall to the ground. I am this heart that beats, this womb that bleeds.

And I'm more than any of the parts of me—I am more than my good parts, and more than my bad ones. I am more than my mistakes. I am more than my memories. I will say these words again and again, like an anthem, like a prayer, until I believe them.

When I was fourteen, my mother told me that there was no such thing as unconditional love. But I am not fourteen, and I am more than my mother's daughter.

AUTHOR'S NOTE

Sugar and spice and everything nice;
That's what girls are made of.

Hearing this nursery rhyme when I was a little girl, I remember feeling smug. I was a girl, and therefore I was made of the good stuff; boys, on the other hand, were made of frogs and snails and puppy dog tails—slimy, icky, dismembered, even. Now, though, I read it differently.

First, I now see that the stuff of girls is meant to be consumed—sugar and spice and everything nice—yummy sweet treats that melt in your mouth.

And it reads to me now as a warning rather than as an assessment. It's an imperative: to be a girl, one must be sweet and delicious. One must be made entirely of everything nice. There is no room in girlhood (and, perhaps, femaleness) for anything else.

But this is not my experience of femaleness. As I grew up, I became distinctly aware that I was not made entirely of sweetness. The things I was made of sometimes disgusted me—my feelings of jealousy and rage, the functions of my body, the things that came out of me on a daily and monthly basis. I was so ashamed of the fact that I was a human body that urinated and defecated that I would pop out a contact lens whenever I needed to go to the bathroom; so deep was my shame that they might know what I was doing in there, I needed the contact lens on my finger as proof that I was going into the restroom for something else, not that.

When I was eleven, a neighborhood girl told me a horror story about a girl whose mother wouldn't let her shave her legs and who was teased constantly by everyone she knew—"Ape Legs," they called her—who one day found a straight edge razor in the sand of the play yard, near the swings. She took it into a bathroom at the park, and when she didn't come back out after many minutes, the group of girls who had teased her followed her in to see what had become of her. They found her perched on the edge of a sink, her leg in front of her a mess of blood and gore as she ran the dirty, rusty razor up her shin again and again, ruining herself in an attempt to be pretty, to be more like what a girl should be.

The girl told me the story with a soft voice and wide eyes, a tone of awful glee propelling each word. Was it a warning, not to shave with dirty razors? It seemed to hairy-legged eleven-year-old me more of a cautionary tale that I shouldn't wait much longer before I rid myself of the unsightly fuzz.

Four years later, legs smooth, tanned, and thin, I walked home from school with a friend whose legs were not as lithe as mine. I was wearing a new floral skirt that flared when I spun, like a little girl's dress, but hugged my hips and butt in a way that wasn't little girlish at all. And looking down at my long, shiny calves, I blurted, "I have perfect legs."

It was a rare moment of confidence and joy in my own flesh, but as soon as the words were spoken, I regretted them. This was not something you said aloud—ever—of your own body. That it was pretty, that it was perfect, that you loved it, even for a second, even just in the right light, the right skirt.

Girls should be made of long legs and long hair, but they should be made of shame, too. Of modesty. Of ignorance. And woe to the girl who isn't.

Recently I read that, when asked how to judge if a sex act has been successful, teen girls list as of primary importance whether the boy enjoyed himself. After that, the markers of successful coupling included: if her body presented as attractive; if nothing embarrassing happened; if the boy contacted her again afterward.

Maybe I should have been shocked that nowhere on this list appeared: if the girl enjoyed herself; if she experienced pleasure; if she achieved orgasm; if she left the experience with the desire to repeat it.

But I wasn't shocked, or surprised, though I did sigh and shake my head and feel so, so sorry—sorry for the girl I once was that my own pleasure and safety weren't priorities to me; sorry to be part of a system that creates girls whose bodies seem to belong to everyone but themselves.

It's not new, our valuation of young female people for how they can serve, satisfy, and satiate. Our girls are both the platter and the meal, and we eat them up—we eat their meat, we lap up their sweetness, we covet and control and consume.

I am angry about all of this, but *What Girls Are Made Of* was not born solely from my anger. It was born equally from my complicity. The ways I submitted to what was expected of me when I was a girl, and the ways I still feel the impulse as a woman to submit. Now, though, what is expected of me is different—as a woman in my forties, it seems that what is expected is for me to fade, to fold inward, and to disappear.

Recently, a boy said something about my daughter that got back to her. She was not pleased. By the time she told me about the incident, she'd already blocked him on social media and told him that what he had said was not respectful. I was absolutely blown away. She asked what I would have done if something like this had happened to me when I was her age; the answer, sadly, was that I would have laughed it off, felt sick to my stomach, and done nothing more.

My freshman year in college, I wandered across the hall from my dorm room and into the room of two boys. It was late morning, and almost everyone else who lived on our floor had gone to class.

I sat on a beanbag; the boys sat on their beds. They were stoned, a little red-eyed, and handsome in the disheveled way boys can be.

I don't know how we got on the topic of sex, but I wasn't surprised that we did. Most conversations, it seemed, went this way.

What did surprise me was when one of the boys opened a drawer and removed a straight edge razor, then straddled me where I sat and pressed the edge of the razor to my neck.

"I could rape you," he said. The other boy, still on his bed, watched with lidded eyes.

I didn't know what to do. I didn't know what to say. I wanted to scream, but on the other hand, I told myself, what if he was joking?

What if I yelled and made a big deal out of it and it turned out that really nothing was wrong?

Minutes passed like that, and I felt the hardening

erection the boy grew as he straddled me, as he dominated me, as he grinned down at me. Eventually he dismounted and I said I had to go to class and I left.

I went to the bathroom and into the farthest shower stall. I sank down to the cold tile floor and curled my knees close to my chest. I pressed my hands into my face and cried as quietly as I could. Even then I didn't want to make too much noise.

How did I come to think that I was a person who wasn't worth screaming for? How was it that the fear of overreacting was stronger than a sense of self-preservation?

I don't write books to teach lessons. I write them to sort through the things that fascinate, scare, repulse, and thrill me. Many of these things rise up like terrible bubbles from my past. I know people are going to read *What Girls Are Made Of* and be unhappy with some of the choices that Nina makes. They are going to tsk and purse their lips, and words like "codependent" and "unlikeable" and "needy" will be attached to her. People will say she is made of bad choices. Parts of her are ugly and mean and gross. Things come out of her— actions and words and excretions—that offend and repulse.

Yes, I will agree. All these things are true. And yet, I love her. I love Nina. I love this book. I love the ugliness and vulnerabilities and fears and shames, all of it. I wrote this book because it rose up out of me. I wrote it for myself.

But, here. You can have it, too. There is enough to share. Eat your fill and consider—what are you made of? Also, remember—you don't owe anyone a slice of your soul. Not your parents. Not your friends. Not your teachers or your lovers or your enemies.

ACKNOWLEDGEMENTS

What Girls Are Made Of was made, well, with the help of lots of women.

First and foremost, I'm deeply grateful for my editor Alix Reid, who trusted my vision and helped me crystalize it. Thank you, Alix.

Suzanne Wertman, CNM, generously answered lists of questions about reproductive health, and Kerri-Lynne Menard explained the procedures for volunteering at an animal shelter.

Kate Healy reminded me to visit the Ecstasy of Saint Teresa while in Rome, and Erin O'Shea told me about the Pear of Anguish.

My sisters Sasha and Mischa were, as always, my first readers, and their enthusiasm means more than they probably know.

Both Martha Brockenbrough and Carrie Mesrobian read early drafts of the book that became *What Girls Are Made Of*, and their insight and encouragement propelled me forward.

I'm indebted to the work of Brandy Colbert, Christa Desir, Sarah McCarry, Laura Ruby, and Erica Lorraine

Scheidt, all novelists who examine the female teenage body in ways that inspired this book.

In addition to these wonderful women, I was aided by a number of good men, including Dean Anderson Ayers, who patiently answered my questions about the practicalities of putting a dog to sleep and what happens to the bodies afterward, Rubin Pfeffer, my steadfast agent, who always returns e-mails quickly and enthusiastically, and Andrew Karre.

Being a full-time writer is a privilege I don't take lightly. Above all, I am indebted to my family, who supports me in all ways.